GRAPES OF WRATH

Boyd Cable

Grapes of wrath

Copyright © 2019 Indo-European Publishing

The present edition is a reproduction of previous publication of this classic work. Minor typographical errors may have been corrected without note, however, for an authentic reading experience the spelling, punctuation, and capitalization have been retained from the original text.

ISBN: 978-1-64439-172-3

CONTENTS

BOYD CABLE—A PREFATORY NOTE

The readers of Boyd Cable's "Between the Lines," "Action Front," and "Doing Their Bit," have very naturally had their curiosity excited as to an author who, previously unheard of, has suddenly become the foremost word-painter of active fighting at the present day, and the greatest "literary discovery" of the War.

Boyd Cable is primarily a man of action; and for half of his not very long life he has been doing things instead of writing them. At the age of twenty he joined a corps of Scouts in the Boer War, and saw plenty of fighting in South Africa. After the close of that war, his life consisted largely of traveling in Great Britain and the principal countries of Europe and the Mediterranean, his choice always leading him from the beaten track. He also spent some time in Australia and in New Zealand, not only in the cities, but in the outposts of civilization, on the edge of the wilderness, both there and in the Philippines, Java, and other islands of the Pacific.

When he travels, Mr. Cable does not merely take a steamer-berth or a railway-ticket and write up his notes from an observation car or a saloon deck. He looks out after a job, and puts plenty of energy into it while he is at it; in fact, so many different things has he done, that he says himself that it is easier to mention the things he has not done than the ones he has. He has been an ordinary seaman, typewriter agent, a steamer-fireman, office-manager, hobo, farmhand, gold prospector, coach-driver, navvy, engine-driver, and many other things. And strangely enough, though he knows so much from practical experience, he has, until recently, never thought of writing down what he has seen.

Before this present War, he was on the staff of a London advertising agency. At the outbreak of hostilities, he offered his services and was accepted in 1914, being one of the first men not in the regular army to get a commission and be sent to the front.

It was his experience as "Forward Officer" (or observation officer in the artillery) that gave him the material which he began to use in "Between the Lines."

In this dangerous and responsible position, his daily life of literally "hairbreadth" escapes afforded him experiences as thrilling as any he has described in his books. On one occasion, for instance, when his position had been "spotted" by enemy sharp-shooters, he got a bullet through his cap, one through his shoulder-strap, one through the inside of his sleeve close to his heart, and fifty-three others near enough for him to hear them pass—all in less than an hour.

After eighteen months of this death-defying work, without even a wound, Mr. Boyd Cable was naturally disgusted at being invalided home on account of stomach trouble; but it was only this enforced leisure that gave him really time to take up writing seriously. As may be remembered, the British Government selected him officially to make the rounds of the munition factories and write an account of what was being done in them, with the purpose of circulating it among the men at the front, to let them see that the workers at home were "doing their bit."

The following letter has just been received from Mr. Boyd Cable by the publishers, and they venture to include it here, entirely without the writer's consent (since that would be impossible to get within the necessary time), and fully realizing that the letter was not written with a view to publication. They feel that it will give the reader an intimate view of the author, such as no amount of description or explanation could do.

"... Many thanks for all the trouble you have taken trying to place my stories in magazines. It certainly is odd that British in U. S. A. are not more interested in the war. I only hope the States won't have one of its own to be interested in, but honestly I expect it within very few years.

I am very glad you like "Grapes of Wrath" and hope the further chapters (which Smith, Elder & Company tell me they have sent you) will equally please. I may not tell you where I am or what I'm doing since the Censor forbids, but may just say that since I came out again I've seen plenty of the Somme "Push" and have been able to make "Grapes of Wrath" the more accurate and up to date in details.

Now we're all awaiting the Spring with full anticipations of going in for the last round and the knock-out to Germany. We're all very confident she can't stand the pace we've set for next year.

We're having some bitter weather—fierce cold and wet and snow, but we're putting up with it, more or less cheered by the assurance that the Huns are feeling it every bit as bad as we are and probably a bit worse.

With all regards and every good wish for the coming year...."

It only remains to add that the importance of Mr. Boyd Cable's work may be judged by the fact that of "Between the Lines" considerably over a hundred thousand copies have been printed in Great Britain alone.

The Publishers

BATTLE HYMN OF THE REPUBLIC

Mine eyes have seen the glory of the coming of the Lord:
He is trampling out the vintage where the grapes of wrath are stored;
He hath loosed the fatal lightning of His terrible swift sword:
His truth is marching on.

I have seen Him in the watch fires of a hundred circling camps;
They have builded Him an altar in the evening dews and damps:
I can read His righteous sentence by the dim and flaring lamps:
His day is marching on.

I have read a fiery gospel, writ in burnished rows of steel:
"As ye deal with My contemners, so with you My grace shall deal";
Let the Hero, born of woman, crush the serpent with His heel!
Since God is marching on!

He has sounded forth the trumpet that shall never call retreat,
He is sifting out the hearts of men before His judgment seat;
Oh! be swift, my soul, to answer Him! be jubilant, my feet!
Our God is marching on.

In the beauty of the lilies Christ was born, across the sea,
With a glory in His bosom that transfigures you and me;
As He died to make men holy, let us die to make men free,
While God is marching on.

He is coming like the glory of the morning on the wave;
He is wisdom to the mighty, He is succor to the brave;
So the world shall be His footstool and the soul of time His slave:
Our God is marching on.

Julia Ward Howe

AUTHOR'S FOREWORD

It is possible that this book may be taken for an actual account of the Somme battle, but I warn readers that although it is in the bulk based on the fighting there and is no doubt colored by the fact that the greater part of it was written in the Somme area or between visits to it, I make no claim for it as history or as an historical account. My ambition was the much lesser one of describing as well as I could what a Big Push is like from the point of view of an ordinary average infantry private, of showing how much he sees and knows and suffers in a great battle, of giving a glimpse perhaps of the spirit that animates the New Armies, the endurance that has made them more than a match for the Germans, the acceptance of appalling and impossible horrors as the work-a-day business and routine of battle, the discipline and training that has fused such a mixture of material into tempered fighting metal.

For the tale itself, I have tried to put into words merely the sort of story that might and could be told by thousands of our men to-day. I hope, in fact, I have so "told the tale" that such men as I have written of may be able to put this book in your hands and say: "This chapter just describes our crossing the open," or "That is how we were shelled," or "I felt the same about my Blighty one."

It may be that before this book is complete in print another, a greater, a longer and bloodier, and a last battle may be begun, and I wish this book may indicate the kind of men who will be fighting it, the stout hearts they will bring to the fight, the manner of faith and assurance they will feel in Victory, complete and final to the gaining of such Peace terms as we may demand.

The Author

In the Field
20th January, 1917

GRAPES OF WRATH

CHAPTER I

TOWARDS THE PUSH

The rank and file of the 5/6 Service Battalion of the Stonewalls knew that "there was another push on" and that they were moving up somewhere into the push; but beyond that and the usual crop of wild and loose-running rumors they knew nothing. Some of the men had it on the most exact and positive authority that they were for the front line and "first over the parapet"; others on equally positive grounds knew that they were to be in reserve and not in the attack at all; that they were to be in support and follow the first line; that there was to be nothing more than an artillery demonstration and no infantry attack at all; that the French were taking over our line for the attack; that we were taking over the French line. The worst of it was that there were so many tales nobody could believe any of them, but, strangely enough, that did not lessen the eager interest with which each in turn was heard and discussed, or prevent each in turn securing a number of supporters and believers.

But all the rumors appeared to be agreed that up to now the push had not begun, so far as the infantry were concerned, and also that, as Larry Arundel put it, "judging by the row the guns are making it's going to be some push when it does come."

The Stonewalls had been marching up towards the front by easy stages for three days past, and each day as they marched, and, in fact, each hour of this last day, the uproar of artillery fire had grown steadily greater and greater, until now the air trembled to the violent concussions of the guns, the shriek and rumble of the shells, and occasionally to the more thrilling and heart-shaking shriek of an enemy shell, and the crash of its burst in our lines.

It was almost sunset when the Stonewalls swung off the road and halted in and about a little orchard. The lines of an encampment— which was intended for no more than a night's bivouac—were laid out, and the men unbuckled their straps, laid off their packs, and sank thankfully to easeful positions of rest on the long grass, waiting until the traveling cookers, which on their journey along the road had been preparing the evening meal, were brought up and discharged of their savory contents. But before the meal was served there came an unpleasant interruption, which boded ill for the safety of the night's camp. A heavy shell rushed overhead, dropped in the field about four hundred yards beyond the camp, burst with a crash and a gush of evil black smoke, a flying torrent of splinters and up-flung earth.

While the men were still watching the slow dispersal of the shell smoke, and passing comments upon how near to them was the line it had taken, another and another shell whooped over them in a prolonged line on the fields beyond. "We seem," said Larry Arundel, "to have chosen a mighty unhealthy position for to-night's rest."

"If the C.O. has any sense," retorted his mate, Billy Simson, "he'll up and off it somewheres out to the flank. We're in the direct line of those crumps, and if one drops short, it is going to knock the stuffin' out of a whole heap of us."

While they were talking an artillery subaltern was seen crossing the road and hurrying towards them. "Where is your C.O.?" he asked, when he came to the nearest group.

"Over in the orchard, sir," said Billy Simson. "I'll show you if you like."

The officer accepted his pilotage, urging him to hurry, and the two hastened to the orchard, and to a broken-down building in the corner of it, where the officers of the battalion were installing a more or less open-air mess.

Billy Simson lingered long enough to hear the Subaltern introduce

2

himself as from a battery in a position across the road amongst some farm buildings, and to say that his Major had sent him over to warn the infantry that the field they were occupying was in a direct line "regularly strafed" by a heavy German battery every few hours.

"My Major said I was to tell you," went on the Subaltern, "that there are one or two old barns and outbuildings on the farm where we have the battery, and that you might find some sort of shelter for a good few of your men in them; and that we can find room to give you and some of the officers a place to shake down for the night."

Simson heard no more than this, but he soon had evidence that the invitation had been accepted. The battalion was warned to "stand by" for a move across the road, and the Colonel and Adjutant, with the Sergeant-Major and a couple of Sergeants, left the orchard and disappeared among the farm buildings, in the company of the gunner Subaltern.

Billy Simson repeated to his particular chums the conversation he had overheard; and the resulting high expectations of a move from the unhealthy locality under the German guns' line of fire, and of a roof over their heads for the night, were presently fulfilled by an order for the battalion to move company by company. "C" Company presently found itself installed in a commodious barn, with ventilation plentifully provided by a huge hole, obviously broken out by a shell burst, in the one corner, and a roof with tiles liberally smashed and perforated by shrapnel fire. But on the whole the men were well content with the change, partly perhaps because being come of a long generation of house-dwellers they had never become accustomed to the real pleasure of sleeping in the open air, and partly because of that curious and instinctive and wholly misplaced confidence inspired by four walls and a roof as a protection against shell fire.

Somewhere outside and very close to them a field battery was in action, and for a whole hour before darkness fell the air pulsed and the crazy buildings about them shook to an unceasing thump and bang from the firing guns, while the intervals were filled with the slightly more distant but equally constant thud and boom of other batteries' fire.

While they were waiting for the evening meal to be served some of the men wandered out and took up a position where they could view closely the guns and gunners at their work. The guns were planted at intervals along a high hedge; the muzzles poked through the leafy screen, and a shelter of leaves and boughs was rigged over each, so as to screen the battery from air observation.

Billy Simson and his three particular chums were amongst the interested spectators. The four men, who were drawn from classes that in pre-war days would have made any idea of friendship or even intercourse most unlikely, if not impossible, had, after a fashion so common in our democratic New Armies, become fast friends and intimates.

Larry Arundel, aged twenty, was a man of good family, who in civilian days had occupied a seat in his father's office in London, with the certain prospect before him of a partnership in the firm. Billy Simson was a year or two older, had been educated in a provincial board school, and from the age of fourteen had served successively as errand boy and counter hand in a little suburban "emporium." The third man, Ben Sneath, age unknown, but probably somewhere about twenty-one to twenty-five, was frankly of the "lower orders"; had picked up a living from the time he was able to walk, in the thousand and one ways that a London street boy finds to his hand. On the roll of "C" Company he was Private Sneath, B, but to the whole of the company—and, in fact, to the whole of the battalion—he was known briefly, but descriptively, as "Pug." Jefferson Lee, the fourth of the quartette, was an unusual and somewhat singular figure in a British battalion, because, always openly proud of his birthplace, he was seldom called by anything but it—"Kentucky," or "Kentuck." His speech, even in the wild jumble of accents and dialects common throughout a mixed battalion, was striking and noticeable for its peculiar softness and slurring intonations, its smooth gentleness, its quiet, drawling level. Being an American, born of many generations of Americans, with no single tie or known relation outside America, he was, in his stained khaki and his place in the fighting ranks of a British regiment, a personal violation of the neutrality of the United States. But the reasons that had brought him from Kentucky to England, with the clear and expressed purpose of enlisting for the war, were very simply explained by him.

"Some of us," he said gently, "never really agreed with the sinking of liners and the murder of women and children. Some of us were a trifle ashamed to be standing out of this squabble, and when the President told the world that we were 'too proud to fight,' I just

4

simply had to prove that it was a statement which did not agree with the traditions of an old Kentucky family. So I came over and enlisted in your army."

The attitude of the four men now as they watched the gunners at work was almost characteristic of each. Larry, who had relatives or friends in most branches of the Service, was able to tell the others something of the methods of modern artillery, and delivered almost a lecturette upon the subject. Billy Simson was frankly bored by this side of the subject, but intensely interested in the noise and the spectacular blinding flash that appeared to leap forth in a twenty-foot wall of flame on the discharge of each gun. Pug found a subject for mirth and quick, bantering jests in the attitudes of the gunners and their movements about the gun, and the stentorian shoutings through a megaphone of the Sergeant-Major from the entrance to a dug-out in the rear of the guns. Lee sat down, leisurely rolled and lit a cigarette, watched the proceedings with interest, and made only a very occasional soft drawled reply to the remarks of the others.

"Do you mean to tell me," said Pug incredulously, breaking in on Arundel's lecture, "that them fellows is shootin' off all them shells without ever seein' what they're firin' at? If that is true, I calls it bloomin' waste."

"They do not see their target," said Arundel, "but they are hitting it every time. You see they aim at something else, and they're told how much to the right or left of it to shoot, and the range they are to shoot at—it is a bit too complicated to explain properly, but it gets the target all right."

"Wot's the bloke with the tin trumpet whisperin' about?" asked Pug. "Looks to me as if he was goin' to be a casualty with a broke blood-vessel."

"Passing orders and corrections of fire to the guns," explained Arundel. "There's a telephone wire from that dug-out up to somewhere in front, where somebody can see the shells falling, and 'phone back to tell them whether they are over or short, right or left."

"It's pretty near as good as a Brock's benefit night," said Billy Simson; "but I'd want cotton wool plugs in my ears, if I was takin' up lodgin's in this street."

The light was beginning to fade by now, but the guns continued to fire in swift rotation, from one end of the battery to the other. They could hear the sharp orders, "One, fire; Two, fire; Three, fire," could see the gunner on his seat beside each piece jerk back the lever. Instantly the gun flamed a sheet of vivid fire, the piece recoiled violently to the rear between the gunners seated to each side of it, and as the breech moved smoothly back to its position, the hand of one gunner swooped rapidly in after it, grabbed the handle and wrenched open the breech, flinging out the shining brass cartridge case, to fall with a clash and jangle on to the trail of the gun and the other empty cases lying round it. The instant the breech was back in place, another man shot in a fresh shell, the breech swung shut with a sharp, metallic clang, the layer, with his eye pressed close to his sight, juggled for a moment with his hands on shiny brass wheels, lifted one hand to drop it again on the lever, shouted "Ready," and sat waiting the order to fire. The motions and the action at one gun were exactly and in detail the motions of all. From end to end of the line the flaming wall leaped in turn from each muzzle, the piece jarred backwards, the empty brass case jerked out and fell tinkling; and before it ceased to roll another shell was in place, the breech clanged home, and the gun was ready again.

Billy Simson spoke to a gunner who was moving past them towards the billets.

"What are you fellows shooting at?" he asked.

"Wire cutting," said the gunner briefly. "We've been at it now without stopping this past four days," and he moved on and left them.

"Wire cutting," said Arundel, "sweeping away the barbed wire entanglements in front of the Boche trench. That's clearing the track we're going to take to-morrow or the next day."

"I hopes they makes a clean job of it," said Pug; "and I hopes they sweep away some of them blasted machine guns at the same time."

"Amen, to that," said Kentucky.

CHAPTER II

THE OVERTURE OF THE GUNS

All that night the men, packed close in their blankets, slept as best they could, but continually were awakened by the roaring six-gun salvos from the battery beside them.

One of the gunners had explained that they were likely to hear a good deal of shooting during the night, "the notion being to bust off six shells every now and again with the guns laid on the wire we were shooting at in daylight. If any Boche crawls out to repair the wire in the dark, he never knows the minute he's going to get it in the neck from a string of shells."

"And how does it work?" asked the interested Arundel.

"First rate," answered the gunner. "Them that's up at the O.P.[1] says that when they have looked out each morning there hasn't been a sign or a symptom of new wire going up, and, of course, there's less chance than ever of repairing in daytime. A blue-bottle fly—let alone a Boche—couldn't crawl out where we're wire-cutting without getting filled as full of holes as a second-hand sieve."

The salvos kept the barnful of men awake for the first hour or two. The intervals of firing were purposely irregular, and varied from anything between three to fifteen minutes. The infantry, with a curious but common indifference to the future as compared to the

---

[1] Observation Post.

present, were inclined to grumble at this noisy interruption of their slumbers, until Arundel explained to some of them the full purpose and meaning of the firing.

"Seein' as that's 'ow it is," said Pug, "I don't mind 'ow noisy they are; if their bite is anything like as good as their bark, it's all helpin' to keep a clear track on the road we've got to take presently."

"Those gunners," said Kentucky, "talked about this shooting match having kept on for four days and nights continuous, but they didn't know, or they wouldn't say, if it was over yet, or likely to be finished soon."

"The wust of this blinkin' show," said Billy Simson, "is that nobody seems to know nothin', and the same people seem to care just about the same amount about anythin'."

"Come off it," said Pug; "here's one that cares a lump. The sooner we gets on to the straff and gets our bit done and us out again the better I'll be pleased. From what the Quarter-bloke says, we're goin' to be kep' on the bully and biscuit ration until we comes out of action; so roll on with comin' out of action, and a decent dinner of fresh meat and potatoes and bread again."

"There's a tidy few," said Billy, "that won't be lookin' for no beef or bread when they comes out of action."

"Go on," said Pug; "that's it; let's be cheerful. We'll all be killed in the first charge; and the attack will be beat back; and the Germans will break our line and be at Calais next week, and bombarding London the week after. Go on; see if you can think up some more cheerfuls."

"Pug is kind of right," said Kentucky; "but at the same time so is Billy. It's a fair bet that some of us four will stop one. If that should be my luck, I'd like one of you," he glanced at Arundel as he spoke, "to write a line to my folks in old Kentucky, just easing them down and saying I went out quite easy and cheerful."

Pug snorted disdainfully. "Seems to me," he said, "the bloke that expec's it is fair askin' for it. I'm not askin' nobody to write off no last dyin' speeches for me, even if I 'ad anybody to say 'em to, which I 'aven't."

"Anyhow, Kentucky," said Arundel, "I'll write down your address, if you will take my people's. What about you, Billy?"

Billy shuffled a little uneasily. "There's a girl," he said, "one girl partikler, that might like to 'ear, and there's maybe two or three others that I'd like to tell about it. You'll know the sort of thing to say. I'll give you the names, and you might tell 'em"—he hesitated a moment—"I know, 'the last word he spoke was Rose—or Gladys, or Mary,' sendin' the Rose one to Rose, and so on, of course."

Arundel grinned, and Pug guffawed openly. "What a lark," he laughed, "if Larry mixes 'em up and tells Rose the last word you says was 'Gladys,' and tells Gladys that you faded away murmurin' 'Good-by, Rose.'"

"I don't see anythin' to laugh at," said Billy huffily. "Rose is the partikler one, so you might put in a bit extra in hers, but it will please the others a whole heap. They don't know each other, so they will never know I sent the other messages, and I'll bet that each of 'em will cart that letter round to show it to all her pals, and they'll cry their eyes out, and have a real enjoyable time over it."

Arundel laughed now. "Queer notions your girls have of enjoyment, Billy," he said.

"I know 'em," insisted Billy; "and I'm right about it. I knew a girl once that was goin' to be married to a chum o' mine, and he ups and dies, and the girl 'ad to take the tru-sox back to the emporium and swop it for mournin'; and the amount of fussin' and cryin'-over that girl got was somethin' amazin', and I bet she wouldn't have missed it for half a dozen 'usbands; and, besides, she got another 'usband easy enough about two months after." He concluded triumphantly, and looked round as if challenging contradiction.

Outside, the battery crashed again, and the crazy building shook about them to the sound. A curious silence followed the salvo, because by some chance the ranked batteries, strung out to either side of them, had chosen the same interval between their firing. Most of the men in the barn had by this time sunk to sleep, but at the silence they stirred uneasily, and many of them woke and raised themselves on their elbows, or sat up to inquire sleepily "What was wrong now?" or "What was the matter?" With the adaptability under which men live in the fire zone, and without which, in fact, they could hardly live and keep their senses, they had in the space of

9

an hour or two become so accustomed to the noise of the cannonade that its cessation had more power to wake them than its noisiest outbursts; and when, after the silence had lasted a few brief minutes, the batteries began to speak again, they turned over or lay down and slid off into heedless sleep.

Somewhere about midnight there was another awakening, and this time from a different cause—a difference that is only in the note and nature of the constant clamor of fire. Throughout the night the guns had practically the say to themselves, bombs and rifles and machine guns alike being beaten down into silence; but at midnight something—some alarm, real or fancied—woke the rifles to a burst of frenzied activity. The first few stuttering reports swelled quickly to a long drum-like roll. The machine guns caught up the chorus, and rang through it in racketing and clattering bursts of fire. The noise grew with the minutes, and spread and spread, until it seemed that the whole lines were engaged for miles in a desperate conflict.

Arundel, awakened by the clamor, sat up. "Is anybody awake?" he asked in low tones, and instantly a dozen voices around him answered.

"Is it the attack, do you suppose?" asked one, and a mild argument arose on the question, some declaring that they—the Stonewalls— would not be left to sleep there in quietness if our line were commencing the push; others maintaining that secrecy was necessary as to the hour planned, because otherwise the Boches would be sure to know it, and be ready for the attack.

"Maybe," some one ventured the opinion, "it's them that's attacking us." But this wild theorist was promptly laughed out of court, it being the settled conviction apparently of his fellows that the Boche would not dare to attack when he knew from the long bombardment that our lines must be heavily held.

As the argument proceeded, Arundel felt a touch on his elbow, heard the soft, drawling voice of Kentucky at his ear.

"I'm going to take a little pasear outside, and just see and hear anything I can of the proceedings."

"Right," said Arundel promptly. "I'm with you; I'm not a bit sleepy, and we might find out something of what it all means."

10

The two slipped on their boots, moved quietly to the door, and stepped outside.

They walked round the end of the barn to where they could obtain a view clear of the building and out towards the front, and stood there some minutes in silence, watching and listening. A gentle rise in the ground and the low crest of a hill hid the trenches on both sides from their view, and along this crest line showed a constant quivering, pulsing flame of pale yellow light, clear and vivid along its lower edge, and showing up in hard, black silhouette every detail of the skyline, every broken tree stump, every ragged fragment of a building's wall, every bush and heap of earth. Above the crest the light faded and vignetted off softly into the darkness of the night, a darkness that every now and then was wiped out to the height of half the sky by a blinding flash of light, that winked and vanished and winked again and again, as the guns on both sides blazed and flung their shells unseeing but unerring to their mark.

Larry and Kentucky heard a call in the battery near them, the quick rush of running feet, a succession of sharp, shouted orders. The next instant, with a crash that made them jump, the six guns of the battery spoke with one single and instantaneous voice. In the momentary gush of flame from the muzzles, and of yellow light, that blotted out all other lights, the two men saw in one quick glimpse the hedge, the leafy screens above the guns, the guns themselves, and the gunners grouped about them. Out to their right, a moment after the darkness had flashed down again over the battery, a neighboring group of guns gave tongue in a rapid succession of evenly spaced reports. This other battery itself was hidden from the two watchers, but because of its nearness, the flashes from it also flung a blinding radiance upward into the night, revealing the outlines of every roof and building, hedge and tree, that stood against the sky.

Their own battery, in answer to a hoarse bellowing from the megaphone of "Section Fire—5 seconds," commenced to pound out a stream of shells from gun after gun. Away to right and left of them the other batteries woke and added their din to the infernal chorus. The shells from other and farther back batteries were rushing and screaming overhead, and dying away in thin wailings and whistlings in the distance.

Another and different note struck in, rising this time from a shrill scream to a louder and louder and more savage roar, and ending

11

with an earth shaking crash and the shriek of flying splinters. A shell had burst a bare hundred yards from where the two stood, hurling some of its fragments over and past them to rap with savage emphasis on the stone and brick of the farm building.

Larry and Kentucky ducked hastily, and ran crouching to the corner of their barn, as another shrill whistle and rush warned them of the approaching shell. This time it burst farther off, and although the two waited a full fifteen minutes, no other shell came near, though along the crest of the sky-line they could see quick flashing burst after burst and thick, billowing clouds of smoke rising and drifting blackly against the background of light beyond the slope.

The tornado of shell fire beat the rifles down again to silence after some minutes. The rolling rifle fire and clatter of machine guns died away gradually, to no more than an occasional splutter, and then to single shots. After that the artillery slowed down to a normal rate of fire, a steady succession of bangs and thuds and rumblings, that, after the roaring tempest of noise of the past few minutes, were no more than comparative quiet.

"I'm glad we came out," said Larry; "it was quite a decent little show for a bit."

Kentucky peered at him curiously. "Did it strike you," he said, "the number of guns there were loosing off in that little show, and that most of those the other side are going to be doing their darnedest to spoil our little show, when it comes the time for us to be over the parapet?"

"I suppose that's so," admitted Larry; "but then, you see, our guns will be doing the same by them, so the game ought to be even so far as that goes."

"The game!" repeated Kentucky reflectively. "I notice quite a few of you boys talk of it as 'a game,' or 'the game'; I wonder why?"

"I don't know," said Larry, "except that—oh, well—just because it is a game, a beastly enough one, I'll admit, but still a game that the best side is going to win."

"The best side——" said Kentucky, "meaning, I suppose, you—us?"

"Why, of course," said Larry, with utter and unquestioning confidence.

12

CHAPTER III

THE EDGE OF BATTLE

The men were awakened early next morning, and turned out, to find a gray, misty dawn. One might have supposed that in the mist it would have been impossible for the gunners to observe and direct any fire, but for all that the artillery on both sides were fairly heavily engaged, and the bangings and thumpings and rumblings rolled away to right and left, until they died down in the distance into the dull, muffled booming of a heavy surf beating on a long beach.

The Stonewalls breakfasted hastily on biscuits, cheese, jam, and tea, were formed up, and moved on to the road. They marched slowly up this in the direction of the front, and presently found the mist clearing away and then dispersing rapidly under the rays of the rising sun. It seemed as if the first beams of sunrise were a signal to the artillery, for the gunfire speeded up and up, until it beat in one long reverberating roar on the trembling air. The firing was not all from our side either; although for the moment none of the enemy shells dropped very close to the Stonewalls, there were enough of them sufficiently close to be unpleasantly startling, and to send their fragments whistling and whining over their hastily ducking heads.

About seven o'clock a new note began to run through the bellowing of the guns—the sharp, more staccato sound of the rifles and machine guns, the distinctive bang of bombs and hand-grenades. The rifle fire, hesitant and spasmodic at first, swelled suddenly to a loud, deep, drumming roll, hung there for several minutes, pitched

13

upward again to a still louder tone, then sank and died away, until it was drowned out in the redoubled clamor of the guns.

The Stonewalls were halted and moved into the side of the road, and squatted lining the ditches and banks, listening to the uproar, discussing and speculating upon its meaning.

"Sounded like an attack, sure thing," said Kentucky, "but whether our side is pushing or being pushed I have not a notion."

"Probably ours," said Larry; "the yarn was going that we were to attack this morning, although some said it was for tomorrow."

"Anyway," said Pug, "if our lot 'as gone over they've either got it in the neck, and 'ad to 'ook it back again, or else they're over the No-Man's-Land, and into the fust line."

"That's what," said Billy Simson. "And 'ark at the bombs and 'and-grenades bustin' off nineteen to the dozen. That means we're bombin' our way along the trenches and chuckin' 'em down into the dugouts."

It was true that the distinctive sound of the bursting bombs had risen again to a renewed activity, and from somewhere further up or down the line the rifle fire commenced again, and rose to one long, continuous full-bodied roar. The sound spread and beat down in rolling waves nearer and nearer, ran outward again on both flanks, continued loud and unceasing.

The Stonewalls were formed up and moved on again, and presently came upon, and marched into, the ruined fragments of a village, with shattered and tumble-down houses lining the sides of the road. They began to notice a new and significant sound, the thin whistling and piping of bullets passing high over their heads, the smack and crack of an occasional one catching some upper portion of the ruined houses past which they marched. Here, too, they began to meet the first of the backwash of battle, the limping figures of men with white bandages about their heads, arms, and bodies; the still forms at full length on the sagging, reddened stretchers. At one of the houses in the village a Red Cross flag hung limp over a broken archway, and through this the procession passed in an ever quickening stream.

The village street rose to the crest of a gentle slope, and when the

14

Stonewalls topped the rise, and began to move down the long gentle decline on the other side, they seemed to step from the outer courts into the inner chambers of war. Men hung about the broken fragments of the buildings; ammunition carts were drawn up in angles and corners of the remaining walls; a couple of ambulances jolted slowly and carefully up the hill towards them; the road was pitted and cratered with shell holes; the trees, that lined both sides of it, trailed broken branches and jagged ends of smashed off trunks, bore huge white scars and patches, and strewed the road with showers of leaves and twigs. The houses of the village, too, on this side of the slope, had been reduced to utter ruin. Only here and there were two-or three-sided portions of a house still standing; the rest were no more than heaped and tangled rubbish-heaps of stone and brick, broken beams and woodwork, shattered pieces of furniture, and litter of red tiles.

By now the bullets were singing and whisking overhead, crackling with vicious emphasis against the trees and walls. And now, suddenly and without the slightest warning, four shells rushed and crashed down upon the road amongst the ruined buildings. The men who had been hanging about in the street vanished hastily into such cover as they could find, and the Stonewalls, tramping steadily down the shell-smashed, rubbish-strewn street, flinched and ducked hastily to the quick rush and crash of another string of shells. An order was passed back, and the column divided into two, half taking one side of the road, and half the other; the rear halting and lying down, while the front moved off by platoons, with some fifty to a hundred yards between each.

A German battery was evidently making a target of this portion of the road, for the shells continued to pound up and down its length. After the sharp burst of one quartette fairly between the ranks of a marching platoon, there was a call for stretchers, and the regimental stretcher-bearers came up at the double, busied themselves for a few minutes about some crumpled forms, lifted them, and moved off along the road back to the Red Cross flag of the dressing station. The shell-swept stretch of road was growing uncomfortably dangerous, and it was with a good deal of relief that the Stonewalls saw their leading platoon turn aside and disappear into the entrance of a communication trench.

"This 'ere," said Pug, with a sigh of satisfaction, "is a blinkin' sight more like the thing; and why them lazy beggars of a Staff 'aven't 'ad this communication trench took back a bit further beats me."

15

"It sure is a comfortable feeling," agreed Kentucky, "to hear those bullets whistling along upstairs, and we safe down below ground level."

The communication trench was very narrow and twisted, and wormed its way for an interminable distance towards the still constant rattle of rifle fire and banging grenades. The men had not the slightest idea what had happened, or what was happening. Some of them had asked questions of the stretcher bearers or of the wounded back in the village, but these it appeared had come from the support trenches and from the firing-line before the uproar of rifle fire had indicated the commencement of an attack by one side or the other. The long, straight, single-file line of Stonewalls moved slowly and with frequent checks and halts for over an hour; then they were halted and kept waiting for a good thirty minutes, some chafing at their inaction, others perfectly content to sit there in the safety of the deep trench. A few men tried to raise themselves and climb the straight sided walls of the trench to the level ground, but the long grass growing there still hid their view, and the few who would have climbed right out on to the level were sharply reprimanded and ordered back by the officers and N.C.O.s; so the line sat or stood leaning against the walls, listening to the unintelligible sounds of the conflict, trying to glean some meaning and understanding of the action's progress from them.

The section of trench where Larry and his friends were waiting was suddenly overcast by a shadow, and the startled men, glancing hastily upward, saw to their astonishment a couple of Highlanders standing over and looking down upon them. One had a red, wet bandage about his head, the other his hose top slit down and dangling about his ankle, and a white bandage wound round the calf of his leg. The two stood for a minute looking down upon the men crouching and squatting in their shelter, on men too astonished for the moment to speak or do aught save gape upwards at the two above them. Somehow, after their relief at escaping from the open into the shelter of the trench, after the doubts and misgivings with which some of them had ventured to raise themselves and peer out above ground level, the angry orders given to them to get back and not expose themselves, after having, in fact, felt themselves for an hour past to be separate only from a sudden and violent death by the depth of their shelter trench, it took their breath away to see two men walking about and standing with apparent unconcern upon a bullet swept level, completely without protection, indifferent to that fact. But they recovered quickly from their amazement.

"Holloa, Jock," Pug called up to them, "what's the latest news in the dispatches? 'Ave we commenced the attack?"

"Commenced? Aye, and gey near finished, as far as we're concerned."

There was a quick chorus of questions to this. "How far had we gone?" "Was the first line taken?" "Was the attack pushing on?" "Had the casualties been heavy?" and a score of other questions.

The two Highlanders bobbed down hastily, as a heavy shell fell with a rolling cr-r-r-ump within a hundred yards of them.

"We've got the first line where we attacked," said one of them after a moment, "and we're pushing on to the second. They say that we have taken the second and third lines down there on the right, but the Huns are counter-attacking, and have got a bit of the third line back. I'm no' sure what's happened on the left, but I'm hearin' the attack was held, and pretty near wiped out. I only ken that our lot is tryin' to bomb up there to the left, and no' makin' much progress."

His companion rose and stepped across the narrow trench.

"Come on, Andy," he said, "we'll awa' back to the dressin' station, and the first train to the North. This is no' just a health resort to be bidin' in. Good luck to you, lads."

"Good luck, so long," chorused the trench after them, and the two vanished from sight.

There was a buzz of excited talk after they had gone—talk that lasted until word was passed back along the trench and the line rose and commenced to stumble onward again.

"I suppose," said Larry, "they'll be moving us up in support. I hope we get out of this beastly trench soon, and see something of what's going on."

Billy Simson grunted. "Maybe we'll see plenty, and maybe a bit too much, when we get out of here," he said, "and it is decently safe down here anyhow."

Pug snorted. "Safe?" he echoed; "no safer than it is above there, by the look of them two Jocks. They don't seem to be worritin' much about it being safe. I believe we would be all right to climb up out of

17

this sewer and walk like bloomin' two-legged humans above ground, instead of crawling along 'ere like rats in a 'Ampton Court maze of drains."

But, whether they liked it or not, the Stonewalls were condemned to spend most of that day in their drains. They moved out at last, it is true, from the communication trench into one of the support trenches, and from this they could catch an occasional narrow glimpse of the battlefield. They were little the wiser for that, partly because the view gave only a restricted vision of a maze of twisting lines of parapets, of which they could tell no difference between British and German; of tangles of rusty barbed wire; and, beyond these things, of a drifting haze of smoke, of puffing white bursts of cotton wool-like smoke from shrapnel, and of the high explosives spouting gushes of heavy black smoke, that leaped from the ground and rose in tall columns with slow-spreading tops. They could not even tell which of these shells were friends' and which were foes', or whether they were falling in the British or the German lines.

Pug was frankly disgusted with the whole performance.

"The people at 'ome," he complained, "will see a blinkin' sight more of this show in the picture papers and the kinema shows than me what's 'ere in the middle of it."

"Don't you fret, Pug," said Larry; "we'll see all we're looking for presently. Those regiments up front must have had a pretty hot strafing, and they're certain to push us up from the supports into the firing-line."

"I don't see what you've got to grumble about," put in Billy Simson; "we're snug and comfortable enough here, and personally I'm not in any hurry to be trottin' out over the open, with the German Army shootin' at me."

"I admit I'm not in any hurry to get plugged myself," drawled Kentucky, "but I've got quite a big mite of sympathy for Pug's feelings. I'm sure getting some impatient myself."

"Anyway," said Pug, "it's about time we 'ad some grub; who's feelin' like a chunk of bully and a pavin'-stone?"

The others suddenly woke to the fact that they also were hungry. Bully beef and biscuits were produced, and the four sat and ate their meal, and lit cigarettes, and smoked contentedly after it, with the roar of battle ringing in their ears, with the shells rumbling and moaning overhead, and the bullets piping and hissing and singing past above their trench.

After their meal, in the close, stagnant air of the trench they began to feel drowsy, and presently they settled themselves in the most comfortable positions possible, and dozed off to sleep. They slept for a good half hour, heedless of all the turmoil about them, and they were roused by a word passed down along the trench.

They rose, and shook the packs into place on their shoulders, tightened and settled the straps about them, patted their ammunition pouches, felt the bayonets slip freely in their scabbards, tried the bolts and action of their rifles, and then stood waiting with a curious thrill, that was made up of expectation, of excitement, of fear, perhaps—they hardly knew what. For the word passed along had been to get ready, that the battalion was moving up into the firing-line.

CHAPTER IV

ACROSS THE OPEN

The order came at last to move, and the men began to work their way along the support trench to the communication trenches which led up into the forward lines.

Up to now the battalion, singularly enough considering the amount of shelling that was going on, had escaped with comparatively few casualties, but they were not to escape much longer. As their line trickled slowly down the communication trench, Pug had no more than remarked on how cheaply they had got off so far, when a six-or eight-inch high-explosive shell dropped with a rolling crump, that set the ground quivering, close to the communication trench. The men began to mend their pace, and to hurry past the danger zone, for they knew well that where one shell fell there was almost a certainty of others falling. A second and a third shell pitched close to the other side of the trench, but the fourth crashed fairly and squarely into the trench itself, blowing out a portion of the walls, killing and wounding a number of men, and shaking down a torrent of loose earth which half choked and filled that portion of the trench. The communication ways, and, indeed, all trenches, are constructed on a principle of curves and zig-zags, designed expressly to localize the effect of a shell bursting in any one portion. Practically every man in this particular section of trench was either killed or wounded, but the rest of the line did not suffer. But the German gunners, having found their target, and having presumably observed their direct hit upon it, had their direction and range exactly, and they proceeded to pound that portion of the trench to pieces, and to make it a matter of desperate hazard for any man to cross the zone covered by their fire. The zone, of course, had to be crossed, the only other alternative being to climb out of the trench and run across the open until the further shelter was reached. There was a still greater hazard attached to this, for the open ground in this locality—as the officers knew—was visible to the German lines, and would expose the men, immediately upon their showing above ground, to a certain sweeping torrent of shrapnel, of machine-gun and rifle fire. So the portion of the battalion which was making its way down that communication trench was set to run the gauntlet of the smashed-in trench, and the shells which continued to arrive— fortunately—with almost methodical punctuality.

The procedure adopted was for the end of the line to halt just short of the fire zone, to wait there, crouched low in the bottom of the trench, until a shell had burst, then to rise and run, scrambling and climbing over the fallen débris, into the comparative safety of the unbroken trench beyond, until the officer who was conducting the timing arrangements thought another shell was due to arrive, and halted the end of the line to wait until the next burst came, after which the same performance was repeated.

Larry and his three chums, treading close on one another's heels, advanced and halted alternately, as the leading portion of the line rushed across or stayed. They came presently to a turn of the trench, where an officer stopped them and bade them lie down, keep as close as they could, and be ready to jump and run when the next shell burst and he gave the word. The four waited through long seconds, their ears straining for the sound of the approaching shell, their eyes set upon the officer.

"Here she comes," said Billy Simson, flattening himself still closer to the trench bottom.

They all heard that thin but ominously rising screech, and each instinctively shrank and tried absurdly to make himself smaller than his size.

"Just a-going to begin," said Larry, with a somewhat forced attempt at lightness of tone.

"Don't you wish you was a bloomin' periwinkle," said Pug, "with a bullet-proof shell?"

There was no time for more. The screech had risen to a rushing bellow, and the next instant the shell dropped with a tumultuous crash, and the air was darkened with a cloud of evil-smelling black smoke, thick, choking, and blinding dust. The four were dazed and shaken with the shock, half-stunned with the thunderclap of noise, and stupefied with the nearness of their escape. But the next instant they were aroused to hear the voice of the officer beside them, calling and shouting to them to get up, to go on, to hurry across.

"Get on!" repeated Pug, scrambling to his knees and feet. "My oath, get on. I wouldn't stop 'ere if I 'ad an invitation to tea with the King 'imself."

"Come, you fellows!" said Larry, and ran with his shoulders stooped, and closely followed by the other three, along a short, unbroken portion of the trench, out into where it was broken down and choked to half its height with the débris of fallen earth and stones. Over this the four clambered and scuffled hastily, to find the trench beyond it wrecked out of semblance to a trench, a tossed and tumbled shallow gutter, with sides fallen in or blown completely out, with huge craters pitting the ground to either side of it, with the black reek and thick dust still curling and writhing and slowly drifting clear from the last explosion. And in that broken welter were the fragments of more than earth or stone; a half-buried patch of khaki, a broken rifle, a protruding boot, were significant of the other and more dreadful fragments buried there.

Larry and the other three did not, to be sure, waste time upon their crossing, but, rapidly as they thought they were moving, they still managed to accelerate their pace as their ears caught the warning sound of another approaching shell, and within a few seconds of hearing its first sound, and the moment when it burst, they had rushed across the remaining portion of the fire-zone, had flung themselves down the sides of the last earth heap, leaped to their feet, and dashed breathlessly into the next unbroken portion of the communication trench. They did not attempt to halt there, but ran on panting and blowing heavily, their packs and haversacks scrubbing one side or the other of the trench, their heads stooped, and their shoulders rounded like men expecting a heavy blow upon their backs. This shell did not pitch into the broken ground where the others had blasted the trench out of any recognizable shape. It burst overhead with a sharp, ear-splitting crack, a puff of thick, yellowish-white smoke, a hail of bullets and flying splinters.

The four men instinctively had half-thrown themselves, half-fallen in the bottom of the trench. It was well they did so, for certainly not all of them could have escaped the huge piece of metal which had been the head of the shell, and which spun down the portion of trench they were in, with a viciously ugly whirr, to bury itself a couple of feet above the footway in the wall, where the trench twisted sharply. It struck close to Pug, so close indeed that when it hit the wall, and then by its own force, breaking down the earth, fell with it into the trench bottom, Pug was able to stretch out his hand and touch it. He gave a sharp yelp of pain and surprise as he did so, whipped his hand in again, and under his armpit.

"Strike me!" he exclaimed, with comical surprise, "the bloomin' thing is red 'ot."

"Come on!" gasped Billy Simson, struggling to his feet again. "This whole blankey corner's too red 'ot for my likin'."

They rose, and pushed hastily on down the winding trench. After that, although they themselves had no especially close shaves, the rest of the line suffered rather severely, for the German gun or guns that had been bombarding the one section of trench now spread their fire and began to pitch high explosives up and down along its whole length. The four had to traverse another short section that had been swept by a low-bursting shrapnel, and after they had passed it, Larry found his knees shaking, and his face wet with cold perspiration.

"Kentuck!" he gulped, "I'm afraid—I'm sorry—I think I'm going to be beastly sick!"

Kentucky, immediately behind him, urged him on.

"Get along, Larry!" he said; "you can't stop here! You'll block the whole line!"

But the line for the moment was blocked. That shell-burst had left few alive in the section of trench, but the two or three it had not killed outright had been dragged clear, and down the trench a little way. Now the men who had taken them out had stopped and laid them down and were shouting vainly—and rather wildly—for stretcher-bearers, and endeavoring—some of the more cool-headed amongst them—to fumble out first field-dressings and apply them to the worst of the many wounds. They halted there, busy, and heedless for the moment of anything else, for a full ten minutes,

23

while the trench behind them filled with men pressing on, shouting angrily, and unknowing the cause of the block, to "Move on there!" to "Get out of the way!"

The end of the line next to the wounded men was forced to try and push forward; the trench was narrow, barely wide enough at its floor-level to accommodate the figures stretched out in it and the men who stooped or knelt over them fumbling at them, rolling and tying the field-dressing bandages upon them; but the men made shift somehow to pass them, striding and straddling over their huddled bodies, squeezing past the men who tried to dress the wounds. These still struggled to complete their task, quite absorbed in it, straightening themselves and flattening their bodies against the trench wall to allow a man to scrape past, stooping again about their work.

"Who has got a spare field-dressing?" or "Give us your field-dressing," was all they took time to say to the men of the passing line, until a wrathful voice above suddenly interrupted them.

One of the officers, fretting at the delay and the slow progress down the trench, had climbed out and run, risking the shells and bullets along the level, to find the cause of the check. He shouted angrily at the men below him:

"Wounded? What's that got to do with it? That's no reason you should block the whole company going forward. Where do you think you're in—a communication trench or a field-dressing-station or a base hospital? Pick those men up—two of you to each man—and carry them along until you can find a place to lay them where you won't choke the whole trench; or carry them right on out of the communication trench."

The wounded men were picked up somehow or anyhow by knees and shoulders, and carried and shuffled and bumped along the winding trench, until they emerged into the old British front-line firing trench.

Along this the Stonewalls now spread and took up their positions as supports for the lines that had gone ahead, and were now over somewhere amongst the German first-line trenches. From here they could look out over the couple of hundred yards' width of what had been the neutral ground, at the old German front-line trench. Beyond its parapet they could see little or nothing but a drifting haze of smoke, but in the open ground between the trenches they could see many figures moving about, and many more lying in still and huddled heaps of khaki. The moving men were for the most part stretcher-bearers, and the Stonewalls were struck with what appeared to them the curious lack of haste and indifference to danger that showed in their movements. During many months, and in many visits to the trenches and spells in the forward fire trench, they had come to regard the neutral ground in daylight as a place whereon no man could walk, or show himself, and live; more than that, they had been taught by strongly worded precept and bitter experience that only to raise a head above the shelter of the parapet, to look for more than seconds at a time over neutral ground, was an invitation to sudden death. It struck them then as a most extraordinary thing that now men should be able to walk about out there, to carry a stretcher in, to hoist it, climbing and balancing themselves and their burden carefully on the parapet, clear and exposed to any chance or aimed bullet.

Kentucky watched some of these groups for a time and then laughed quietly.

"Well!" he drawled, "I've been kind of scared stiff for days past at the thought of having to bolt across this open ground, and here I come and find a bunch of fellows promenading around as cool and unconcerned as if there weren't a bullet within a mile of them."

"I was thinkin' just the same thing," agreed Pug, who was beside him, and looking with interest and curiosity over the open ground; "but if there ain't many bullets buzzin' about 'ere now you can bet there was not long ago. There's a pretty big crowd of ours still lying na-poo-ed out there."

But the ground was still far from being as safe as for the moment it appeared. The German artillery and the machine-gunners were evidently too busily occupied upon the more strenuous work of checking the advance, or did not think it worth while wasting ammunition upon the small and scattered targets presented by the stretcher-bearers. But when a regiment which prolonged the line to the left of the Stonewalls climbed from the trench, and began to advance by companies in open order across the neutral ground, it was a different story.

An exclamation from Pug and a soft whistle from Kentucky brought Larry to the parapet beside them, and the three watched in

25

fascinated excitement the attempt of the other regiment to cross the open, the quick storm of shells and bullets that began to sweep down upon them the moment they showed themselves clear of the parapet. They could see plainly the running figures, could see them stumble and fall, and lie still, or turn to crawl back to cover; could see shell after shell burst above the line, or drop crashing upon it; could see even the hail of bullets that drummed down in little jumping spurts of dust about the feet of the runners.

A good many more of the Stonewalls were watching the advance, and apparently the line of their heads, showing over the parapet, caught the attention of some German machine-gunners. The heads ducked down hastily as a stream of bullets commenced to batter and rap against the parapet, sweeping it up and down, down and up its length.

"Doesn't seem quite as safe as we fancied," said Kentucky.

"I don't think!" said Pug.

"Anyway," said Larry, "it's our turn next!"

He was right, for a few minutes later their officer pushed along and told them to "Stand by," to be ready to climb out when the whistle blew, and to run like blazes for the other side.

"We'll run all right," said Pug to the others, "if them jokers lets us," and he jerked his head upwards to the sound of another pelting sweep of bullets driving along the face of the parapet above them.

Before the whistle blew as the signal for them to leave the trench, an order was passed along that they were to go company by company, A being first, B second, and C third. A couple of minutes later A Company, out on the right of the battalion, swarmed suddenly over the parapet and, spreading out to open order as they went, commenced to jog steadily across the flat ground. Immediately machine-gun fire at an extreme range began to patter bullets down amongst the advancing men, and before they were quarter-way across the "Fizz-Bang" shells also began to smash down along the line, or to burst over it. There were a number of casualties, but the line held on steadily. Some of the men of the remaining companies were looking out on the advance, but the officers ordered them to keep down, and under cover.

In C Company a lieutenant moved along the line, ordering the men down, and repeating the same sentences over and over again as he passed along.

"Keep down until you get the word; when we start across, remember that, if a man is hit, no one is to stop to pick him up; a stretcher-bearer will see to him."

"That's all right!" said Larry to the others, when the officer had passed after repeating his set sentences, "but I vote we four keep together, and give each other a hand, if we can."

"'Ear, 'ear!" said Pug. "Any'ow, if any of us stops one, but isn't a complete wash-out, the others can lug 'im into any shell 'ole that's 'andy, and leave 'im there."

"We'll call that a bargain," said Kentucky briefly. They sat fidgeting for a few seconds longer, hearing the rush and crash of the falling shells, the whistle and smack of the bullets on the open ground beyond them.

"I'm going to have a peep," said Larry suddenly, "just to see how 'A' is getting on."

He stood on the fire step, with his head stooped cautiously below the level of the parapet; then, raising it sharply, took one long, sweeping glance, and dropped down again beside his fellows.

"They're nearly over," he said. "There's a lot of smoke about, and I can't see very clear, but the line doesn't look as if it had been very badly knocked about."

"There goes 'B,'" said Billy Simson, as they heard the shrill trill of a whistle. "Our turn next!"

"That open ground is not such a healthy resort as we thought it a few minutes ago," said Larry. "Personally, I sha'n't be sorry when we're across it."

He spoke in what he strove to make an easy and natural voice, but somehow he felt that it was so strained and unnatural that the others would surely notice it. He felt horribly ashamed of that touch of faintness and sickness back in the communication trench, and began to wonder nervously whether the others would think he was a coward, and funking it; still worse, began to wonder whether actually they would be right in so thinking. He began to have serious

27

doubts of the matter himself, but, if he had known it, the others were feeling probably quite as uncomfortable as himself, except possibly Pug, who had long since resigned himself to the comforting fatalism that if his name were written on the bullet it would find him. If not, he was safe.

None of the four looked to see how "B" Company progressed. They were all beginning to feel that they would have to take plenty of chances when it came their turn to climb the parapet, and that it was folly to take an extra risk by exposing themselves for a moment before they need.

A shout came from the traverse next to them.

"Get ready, 'C' Company; pass the word!"

The four stood up, and Larry lifted his voice, and shouted on to the next traverse.

"Get ready, 'C'; pass the word!"

"Don't linger none on the parapet, boys," said Kentucky. "They've probably got their machine gun trained on it."

The next instant they heard the blast of a whistle, and a shout rang along the line.

"Come on, 'C'; over with you!"

The four leaped over the parapet, scrambling and scuffling up its broken sides.

Near the top Pug exclaimed suddenly, grasped wildly at nothing, collapsed and rolled backward into the trench. The other three half-halted, and looked round.

"Come on," said Kentucky; "he's safest where he is, whether he's hurt much or little."

The three picked their way together out through the remains of the old barbed-wire entanglements, and began to run across.

"Open out! Open out!" the officers were shouting, and a little reluctantly, for the close elbow-touching proximity to each other gave a comforting sense of helpfulness and confidence, they

28

swerved a yard or two apart, and ran on steadily. The bare two hundred yards seemed to stretch to a journey without end; the few minutes they took in crossing spun out like long hours.

Several times the three dropped on their faces, as they heard the warning rush of a shell. Once they half-fell, were half-thrown down by the force of an explosion within twenty yards of them. They rose untouched, by some miracle, and, gasping incoherent inquiries to one another, went on again. Over and over again fragments from the shells bursting above the line rattled down upon the ground amongst their feet. At least two or three times a shell bursting on the ground spattered them with dust and crumbs of earth; the whole way across they were accompanied by the drumming bullets that flicked and spurted little clouds of dust from the ground about them, and all the time they were in the open they were fearfully conscious of the medley of whining and singing and hissing and zipping sounds of the passing bullets. They knew nothing of how the rest of the line was faring. They were too taken up with their own part, were too engrossed in picking a way over the broken shell-cratered ground, past the still khaki forms that lay dotted and sprawled the whole way across.

There was such a constant hail and stream of bullets, such a succession of rushing shells, of crashing explosions, such a wild chaos of sounds and blinding smoke and choking reek, that the whole thing was like a dreadful nightmare; but the three came at last, and unharmed, to the chopped and torn-up fragments of the old German wired defenses, tore through them somehow or anyhow, leaped and fell over the smashed-in parapet, and dropped panting and exhausted in the wrecked remains of the German trench. It was some minutes before they took thought and breath, but then it was evident that the minds of all ran in the same groove.

"I wonder," said Larry, "if Pug was badly hit?"

"I've no idea," said Kentucky. "He went down before I could turn for a glimpse of him."

"I don't suppose it matters much," said Billy Simson gloomily. "He's no worse off than the rest of us are likely to be before we're out of this. Seems to me, by the row that's goin' on over there, this show is gettin' hotter instead of slackin' off."

CHAPTER V

ON CAPTURED GROUND

"I wonder what the next move is?" said Larry. "I don't fancy they will leave us waiting here much longer."

"Don't you suppose," asked Kentucky, "we'll wait here until the other companies get across?"

"Lord knows," said Larry; "and, come to think of it, Kentuck, has it struck you how beastly little we do know about anything? We've pushed their line in a bit, evidently, but how far we've not an idea. We don't know even if their first line is captured on a front of half a mile, or half a hundred miles; we don't know what casualties we've got in our own battalion, or even in our own company, much less whether they have been heavy or light in the whole attack."

"That's so," said Kentucky; "although I confess none of these things is worrying me much. I'm much more concerned about poor old Pug being knocked out than I'd be about our losing fifty per cent. of half a dozen regiments."

Billy Simson had taken the cork from his water-bottle, and, after shaking it lightly, reluctantly replaced the cork, and swore violently.

"I've hardly a mouthful left," he said. "I'm as dry as a bone now, and the Lord only knows when we'll get a chance of filling our water-bottles again."

"Here you are," said Larry; "you can have a mouthful of mine; I've hardly touched it yet."

Orders came down presently to close in to the right, and in obedience the three picked up their rifles and crept along the trench. It was not a pleasant journey. The trench had been very badly knocked about by the British bombardment; its sides were broken in, half or wholly filling the trench; in parts it was obliterated and lost in a jumble of shell craters; ground or trench was littered with burst sandbags, splintered planks and broken fascines, and every now and again the three had to step over or past bodies of dead men lying huddled alone or in groups of anything up to half a dozen. There were a few khaki forms amongst these dead, but most were in the German gray, and most had been killed very obviously and horribly by shell or bomb or grenade.

"They don't seem to have had many men holding this front line," remarked Larry, "or a good few must have bolted or surrendered. Doesn't seem as if the little lot here could have done much to hold the trench."

"Few men and a lot of machine guns, as usual, I expect," said Kentucky. "And if this is all the trench held they claimed a good bunch of ours for every one of theirs, if you judge by the crowd of our lot lying out there in the open."

The three were curiously unmoved by the sight of these dead—and dead, be it noted, who have been killed by shell fire or bomb explosions might as a rule be expected to be a sight upsetting to the strongest nerves. They were all slightly and somewhat casually interested in noting the mode and manner of death of the different men, and the suspicion of professional jealousy evinced by a remark of Billy Simson's was no doubt more or less felt by all, and all were a little disappointed that there was not more evidence of the bayonet having done its share. "The bloomin' guns seem to have mopped most o' this lot," said Billy. "An' them fellers that charged didn't find many to get their own back on." They were all interested, too, in the amount of damage done by the shells to the trench, in the methods of trench construction, in the positions and state of the dug-outs. And yet all these interests were to a great extent of quite a secondary nature, and the main theme of their thoughts was the bullets whistling over them, the rush and crump and crash of the shells still falling out on the open, the singing and whirring of their splinters above the trench. They moved with heads stooped and bodies half-crouched, they hurried over the earth heaps that blocked the trench, and in crossings where they were more exposed, halted and crouched still lower under cover when the louder and rising roar of a shell's approach gave warning that it was falling near.

When they had moved up enough to be in close touch with the rest of the company and halted there, they found themselves in a portion of trench with a dug-out entrance in it. The entrance was almost closed by a fall of earth, brought down apparently by a bursting shell, and when they arrived they found some of the other men of the company busy clearing the entrance. "Might be some soo-veniers down 'ere," one of the men explained. "An', any'ow, we'd be better down below an' safer out o' reach o' any shell that flops in while we're 'ere," said another.

"Suppose there's some bloomin' 'Uns still there, lyin' doggo," suggested Billy Simson. "They might plunk a shot at yer when you goes down."

"Shouldn't think that's likely," said Larry. "They would know that if they did they'd get wiped out pretty quick after."

"I dunno," said one of the men. "They say their officers an' their noospapers 'as 'em stuffed so full o' fairy tales about us killing all prisoners that they thinks they're goin' to get done in anyhow, an' might as well make a last kick for it. I vote we chuck a couple o' bombs down first, just to make sure."

Everybody appeared to think this a most natural precaution to take, and a proposal in no way cruel or brutal; although, on the other hand, when Larry, with some feeling that it was an unsporting arrangement, suggested that they call down first and give any German there a chance to surrender, everybody quite willingly accepted the suggestion. So work was stopped, and all waited and listened while Larry stuck his head into the dark opening and shouted with as inquiring a note as he could put into his voice the only intelligible German he knew, "Hi, Allemands, kamerad?" There was no answer, and he withdrew his head. "I don't hear anything," he said; "but perhaps they wouldn't understand what I meant. I'll just try them again in French and English." He poked his head in again, and shouted down first in French and then in English, asking if there was anybody there, and did they surrender. He wound up with a repetition of his inquiring, "Kamerad, eh? kamerad?" but this time withdrew his head hurriedly, as an unmistakable answer came up to him, a muffled, faraway sounding "Kamerad." "There's some of them there, after all," he said, excitedly, "and they're shouting

32

'Kamerad,' so I suppose they want to surrender all right. Let's clear away enough of this to get them out. We'll make 'em come one at a time with their hands well up."

There was great excitement in the trench, and this rather increased when a man pushed round the traverse from the next section with the news that some Germans had been found in another dugout there. "They're singin' out that they want to kamerad," he said; "but we can't persuade 'em to come out, an' nobody is very keen on goin' down the 'ole after 'em. We've passed the word along for an officer to come an' see what 'e can do with 'em."

"Let's hurry up and get our gang out," said Larry enthusiastically, "before the officer comes"; and the men set to work with a will to clear the dugout entrance. "It's rather a score for the Stonewalls to bring in a bunch of prisoners," said one of the men. "We ought to search all these dugouts. If there's some in a couple of these holes it's a fair bet that there's more in the others. Wonder how they haven't been found by the lot that took the trench?"

"Didn't have time to look through all the dugouts, I suppose," said Larry. "And these chaps would lie low, thinking the trench might be retaken. I think that hole is about big enough for them to crawl out. Listen! They're shouting 'Kamerad' again. Can't you hear 'em?"

He looked down the dark stairway of the entrance and shouted "Kamerad" again, and listened for the reply. "I wonder if the door is blocked further down," he said. "I can hear them shout, but the sound seems to be blocked as if there was something between us and them still. Listen again."

This time they all heard a faint shout, "Kamerad. Hier kom. Kamerad."

"Hier kom—that means come here, I fancy," said Larry. "But why don't they hier kom to us? Perhaps it is that they're buried in somehow and want us to get them out. Look here, I'm going to crawl down these steps and find out what's up."

He proceeded to creep cautiously down the low and narrow passage of the stair, when suddenly he saw at the stair foot the wandering flash of an electric torch and heard voices calling plainly in English to "Come out, Bochie. Kamerad."

The truth flashed on Larry, and he turned and scuttled back up the stair gurgling laughter. "It's some of our own lot down there," he chuckled to the others. "This dug-out must have another entrance in the next traverse, and we and the fellows round there have been shouting down the two entrances at each other. Hold on now and listen and hear them scatter." He leaned in at the entrance again, and shouted loudly. "As you won't come out and surrender, Boche, we're going to throw some bombs down on you." He picked up a heavy stone from the trench bottom and flung it down the steps. There was a moment of petrified silence, then a yell and a scuffling rush of footsteps from the darkness below, while Larry and the others sat and rocked with laughter above. They pushed round the traverse just as a couple of badly scared and wholly amazed Stonewalls scrambled up from the dug-out, and commenced a voluble explanation that "the blighters is chuckin' bombs, ... told us in English, good plain English, too, they was goin' to 'cos we wouldn't surrender."

Just then an officer pushed his way along to them, and the joke was explained with great glee by Larry and the men from the other part of the trench. Every one thought it a huge joke, and laughed and cracked jests, and chuckled over the episode. Kentucky listened to them with some wonder. He had thought that in the past months of peace and war he had come to know and understand these comrades of his fairly well. And yet here was a new side in their many-sided characters that once more amazed him. A couple of dead Germans sprawled in the bottom of the trench a yard or two from them; their own dead lay crowded thick on the flat above; the bullets and shells continued to moan and howl overhead, to rush and crash down close by, the bullets to pipe and whistle and hiss past and over; while only a few hundred yards away the enemy still fought desperately to hold their lines against our attacks, and all the din of battle rolled and reverberated unceasingly. And yet the men in that trench laughed and joked. They knew not the moment when one of those shells falling so close outside might smash into the trench amongst them, knew that all of those there would presently be deep in the heart of the battle and slaughter that raged so close to them, knew for a certainty that some of them would never come out of it; and yet—they laughed. Is it any wonder that Kentucky was amazed?

And they continued to chuckle and poke fun at the two who had been the butt of the jest and had run from the flung stone, continued even as they began to move slowly along the ruined trench that led towards the din of the fighting front lines.

34

CHAPTER VI

TAKING PUNISHMENT

"C" Company of the Stonewalls progressed slowly for some distance up the communication trench, with the whistling of bullets growing faster the nearer they approached to the firing line. This trench too had been badly damaged previous to the attack by the British artillery, and the cover it afforded to the crawling line of men was frequently scanty, and at times was almost nil. There were one or two casualties from chance bullets as men crawled over the débris of wrecked portions of the trench, but the line at last reached what had been one of the German support trenches, and spread along it, without serious loss.

This trench had been reversed by our Engineers, that is to say, the sandbags and parapet on what had been its face, looking towards the British line, had been pulled down and re-piled on the new front of the trench, which now looked towards the ground still held by the Germans. The trench was only some three to four hundred yards behind what was here the most advanced British line, the line from which some of our regiments were attacking, and in which they were being attacked. Practically speaking, therefore, the Stonewalls knew their position was well up on the outer fringe of the infantry fighting, and through it swirled constantly eddies from the firing line in the shape of wounded men and stretcher-bearers, and trickling but constantly running streams of feeders to the fighting—ammunition carriers, staggering under the weight of ammunition boxes and consignments of bombs and grenades; regimental stretcher-bearers returning for fresh loads; ration parties carrying up food and water. There were still communication trenches leading

35

from the Stonewalls' position to the firing line, but because these had been and still were made a regular target by the German guns, had been smashed and broken in beyond all real semblance of cover or protection, and brought their users almost with certainty under the bursting shrapnel or high explosive with which the trench was plastered, most of the men going up or coming back from the forward trench, and especially if they were laden with any burden, preferred to take their chance and make the quicker and straighter passage over the open ground.

The daylight was beginning to fade by now, the earlier because dark clouds had been massing, and a thin misty drizzle of rain had begun to fall; but although it was dusk there was no lack of light in the fighting zone. From both the opposing trenches soaring lights hissed upwards with trailing streams of sparks, curved over, burst into vivid balls of brilliant light, and floated slowly and slantingly downwards to the ground.

The Stonewalls could see—if they cared to look over their parapet— this constant succession of leaping, soaring, and sinking lights, the dancing black shadows they threw, and the winking spurts of fiery orange flame from the rifle muzzles and from the bursting grenades, while every now and again a shell dropped with a blinding flash on or behind one or other of the opposing parapets. There were not many of the Stonewalls who cared to lift their heads long enough to watch the blazing display and the flickering lights and shadows. The position of their trench was slightly higher than the front line held by the Germans, and as a result there was always a hissing and whizzing of bullets passing close overhead, a smacking and slapping of others into their parapet and the ground before it; to raise a head above the parapet was, as the men would have said, "Askin' for it," and none of them was inclined needlessly to do this. But the other men who passed to and fro across their trench, although they no doubt liked their exposure as little as the Stonewalls did, climbed with apparent or assumed indifference over the parapet and hurried stooping across the open to the next trench, or walked back carefully and deliberately, bearing the stretcher laden with the wounded, or helping and supporting the casualties who were still able in any degree to move themselves.

The Stonewalls were given no indication of the time they were to remain there, of when or if they were to be pushed up into the forward trench. The thin rain grew closer and heavier, a chill wind began to blow, setting the men shivering and stamping their feet in

36

a vain attempt to induce warmth. Some of them produced food from their haversacks and ate; almost all of them squatted with rounded shoulders and stooping heads and smoked cigarettes with hands curved about them to hold off the rain, or pipes lit and turned upside down to keep the tobacco dry. They waited there for hours, and gradually, although the sounds of fighting never ceased on their front, the rolling thunder that had marked the conflict during the day died down considerably as the night wore on, until it became no more than a splutter and crackle of rifle fire, a whirring and clattering outburst from some distant or near machine gun, the whoop and rush and jarring burst of an occasional shell on the British or German lines.

At intervals the fight flamed upward into a renewed activity, the rifle fire rose rolling and drumming, the machine guns chattered in a frenzy of haste; the reports of the bursting bombs and grenades followed quickly and more quickly upon each other. Invariably the louder outburst of noise roused the guns on both sides to renewed action. The sky on both sides winked and flamed with flashes that came and went, and lit and darkened across the sky, like the flickering dance of summer lightning. The air above the trenches shook again to the rush of the shells; the ground about and between the front lines blazed with the flashes of the bursts, was darkened and obscured by the billowing clouds of smoke and the drifting haze of their dissolving. Invariably, too, the onslaught of the guns, the pattering hail of their shrapnel, the earth-shaking crash of the high explosives, reduced almost to silence the other sounds of fighting, drove the riflemen and bomb-throwers to cover, and so slackened off for a space the fierceness of the conflict.

To the Stonewalls the night dragged with bitter and appalling slowness; they were cramped and uncomfortable; they were wet and cold and miserable. The sides of the trench, the ground on which they sat, or lay, or squatted, turned to slimy and sticky mud, mud that appeared to cling and hold clammily and unpleasantly to everything about them, their boots and puttees, the skirts of their coats, their packs and haversacks, their hands and rifles and bayonets, and even to their rain-wet faces.

Long before the dawn most of the men were openly praying that they would soon be pushed up into the front rank of the fighting, not because they had any longing or liking for the fight itself, not that they had—any more than any average soldier has—a wish to die or to take their risks, their heavy risks, of death or wounds, but simply because they were chilled to the bone with inaction, were wholly and utterly and miserably wet and uncomfortable, were anxious to go on and get it over, knowing that when they had been in the front line for a certain time, had been actively fighting for so long, and lost a percentage of their number in casualties, they would be relieved by other regiments, would be withdrawn, and sent back to the rear. That sending back might mean no more than a retirement of a mile or two from the front trench, the occupation of some other trench or ditch, no less wet and uncomfortable than the one they were in; but, on the other hand, it might mean their going back far enough to bring them again into touch with the broken villages in the rear, with houses shattered no doubt by shell fire but still capable of providing rough and ready-made shelter from the rain, and, a boon above all boons, wood for fires, with crackling, leaping, life-giving flames and warmth, with the opportunity of boiling mess-tins of water, of heating tinned rations, and of making scalding hot tea.

There might be much to go through before such a heaven could be reached. There were certainly more long hours in the hell of the forward line, there was black death and burning pain, and limb and body mutilation for anything up to three-fourths of their number, to be faced. There were sleeting rifle bullets, and hailing storms from the machine guns, shattering bombs and grenades, rending and tearing shrapnel and shell splinters, the cold-blooded creeping murder of a gas attack perhaps; the more human heat and stir of a bayonet charge; but all were willing, nay, more, all would have welcomed the immediate facing of the risks and dangers, would have gladly taken the chance to go on and get it over, and get back again—such of them as were left—to where they could walk about on firm ground, and stretch their limbs and bodies to sleep in comparative dryness. But no order came throughout the night, and they lay and crouched there with the rain still beating down, with the trench getting wetter and muddier and slimier about them, with their bodies getting more numbed, and their clothing more saturated; lay there until the cold gray of the dawn began to creep into the sky, and they roused themselves stiffly, and with many groans, to meet what the new day might bring forth to them.

The day promised to open badly for the Stonewalls. As the light grew, and became sufficiently strong for the observation of artillery fire, the guns recommenced a regular bombardment on both sides.

From the first it was plain that the support trench occupied by the Stonewalls had been marked down as a target by the German gunners. The first couple of shells dropped on the ground behind their trench and within fifty yards of it, sending some shrieking fragments flying over their heads, spattering them with the mud and earth outflung by the explosions. Another and then another fell, this time in front of their trench, and then one after another, at regular intervals of two to three minutes, a heavy high explosive crashed down within a yard or two of either side of the trench, breaking down the crumbling sides, blowing in the tottering parapet, half-burying some of the men in a tumbling slide of loose, wet earth and débris; or falling fairly and squarely in the trench itself, killing or wounding every man in the particular section in which it fell, blasting out in a fountain of flying earth and stones and mud the whole front and back wall of the trench, leaving it open and unprotected to the searching shrapnel that burst overhead and pelted down in gusts along the trench's length.

The Stonewalls lay and suffered their cruel punishment for a couple of hours, and in that time lost nearly two hundred men, many of them killed, many more of them so cruelly wounded they might almost be called better dead; lost their two hundred men without stirring from the trench, without being able to lift a finger in their own defense, without even the grim satisfaction of firing a shot, or throwing a bomb, or doing anything to take toll from the men who were punishing them so mercilessly for those long hours.

Larry, Kentucky, and Simson lay still, and crouched close to the bottom of the trench, saying little, and that little no more than expressions of anger, of railing against their inaction, of cursings at their impotence, of wondering how long they were to stick there, of how much longer they could expect to escape those riving shells, that pounded up and down along the trench, that sent shiverings and tremblings through the wet ground under them, that spat at them time and again with earth and mud and flying clods and stones. In those two hours they heard the cries and groans that followed so many times the rending crash and roar of the shell's explosion on or about the trench; the savage whistling rush and crack of the shrapnel above them, the rip and thud of the bullets across trench and parapet. They saw many wounded helped and many more carried out past them to the communication trench that led back to the rear and to the dressing-stations. For all through the two hours, heedless of the storm of high explosive that shook and battered the trench to pieces, the stretcher-bearers worked, and picked up the casualties, and sorted out the dead and the dying from the wounded, and applied hasty but always neat bandages and first field-dressings, and started off those that could walk upon their way, or laid those who were past walking upon their stretchers and bore them, staggering and slipping and stumbling, along the muddy trench into the way towards the rear.

"I wonder," said Larry savagely, "how much longer we're going to stick here getting pounded to pieces. There won't be any of the battalion left if we're kept here much longer."

"The front line there has been sticking longer than us, boy," said Kentucky, "and I don't suppose they're having any softer time than us."

"I believe it's all this crowd trampin' in an' out of our trench that's drawin' the fire. They ought to be stopped," said Billy Simson indignantly. "Here's some more of 'em now.... Hi, you! Whatjer want to come crawlin' through this way for? Ain't there any other way but trampin' in an' out on top of us 'ere?"

The couple of mud-bedaubed privates who had slid down into the trench and were hoisting an ammunition-box on to the parapet stopped and looked down on Billy crouching in the trench bottom. "Go'n put yer 'ead in a bag," said one coarsely. "Of course, if you says so, me lord dook," said the other with heavily sarcastic politeness, "we'll tell the C.O. up front that you objects to us walkin' in your back door an' out the front parlor; an' he must do without any more ammunition 'cos you don't like us passing through this way without wipin' our feet on the mat."

"Oh, come on an' leave it alone," growled the first, and heaved himself over the parapet. The other followed, but paused to look back at Billy. "Good job the early bird don't 'appen to be about this mornin'," he remarked loudly, "or 'e might catch you," and he and his companion vanished.

"What's the good of grousing at them, Billy?" said Larry. "They've got to get up somehow." He was a little inclined to be angry with Billy, partly because they were all more or less involved in the foolish complaint, and partly no doubt just because he was ready to be angry with any one or anything.

40

"Why do they all come over this bit of trench, then?" demanded Billy. "And I'm damned if 'ere ain't more of 'em. Now wot d'you suppose he's playin' at?"

"They're Gunners," said Larry, "laying a telephone wire out, evidently."

A young officer, a Second Lieutenant, and two men crept round the broken corner of the trench. One of the men had a reel of telephone wire, which he paid out as he went, while the other man and the officer hooked it up over projections in the trench wall or tucked it away along the parts that offered the most chance of protection. The officer turned to the three men who crouched in the trench watching them.

"Isn't there a communication trench somewhere along here?" he asked, "one leading off to the right to some broken-down houses?"

"We don't know, sir," said Larry. "We haven't been further along than this, or any further up."

"The men going up to the front line all say the communication trenches are too badly smashed, and under too hot and heavy a fire to be used," said Kentucky; "most of them go up and down across the open from here."

"No good to me," said the officer. But he stood up and looked carefully out over the ground in front.

"No good to me," he repeated, stepping back into the trench. "Too many shells and bullets there for my wire to stand an earthly. It would be chopped to pieces in no time."

"Look out, sir," said Larry hurriedly; "there comes another one."

The officer and his two men stooped low in the trench, and waited until the customary rush had ended in the customary crash.

"That," said the officer, standing up, "was about a five-point-nine H.E., I reckon. It's mostly these six-and eight-inch they have been dumping down here all the morning."

He and his men went on busily with their wiring, and before they moved off into the next traverse he turned to give a word of warning to the infantrymen to be careful of his wire, and to jump on any one they saw pulling it down or trampling on it.

41

"Lots of fellows," he said, "seem to think we run these wires out for our own particular benefit and amusement, but they howl in a different tune if they want the support of the guns and we can't give it them because our wire back to the battery is broken."

The three regarded the slender, wriggling wire with a new interest after that, and if the rest of the trench full of Stonewalls were as zealous in their protection as they were, there was little fear of the wire being destroyed, or even misplaced, by careless hands or feet.

Billy Simson cursed strenuously a pair of blundering stretcher-bearers when one of their elbows caught the wire and pulled it down. "'Ow d'yer suppose," he demanded, "the Gunners' Forward Officer is goin' to tell 'is guns back there to open fire, or keep on firin', if yer go breakin' up 'is blinkin' wire?" And he crawled up and carefully returned the wire to its place.

"Look out," he kept saying to every man who came and went up and down or across the trench. "That's the Gunners' wire; don't you git breakin' it, or they can't call up to git on with the shellin'.'"

About two or three hours after dawn the German bombardment appeared to be slackening off, but again within less than half an hour it was renewed with a more intense violence than ever. The Stonewalls' trench was becoming hopelessly destroyed, and the casualties in the battalion were mounting at serious speed.

"Hotter than ever, isn't it?" said Larry, and the other two assented.

"We're lucky to 'ave dodged it so far," said Billy Simson; "but by the number o' casualties we've seen carted out, the battalion is coppin' it pretty stiff. If we stop 'ere much longer, there won't be many of us left to shove into the front line, when we're needed."

"D'ye notice," said Kentucky, "that the rifle firing and bombing up in front seems to have eased off a bit, and the guns are doing most of the work?"

"Worse luck," said Larry, "I'd sooner have the bullets than the shells any day."

"Ar'n't you the Stonewalls?" suddenly demanded a voice from above them, and the three looked up to see a couple of men standing on the rearward edge of the trench.

"Yes, that's right," they answered in the same breath, and one of the men turned and waved his hand to the rear.

"Somebody is lookin' for you," he remarked, jumping and sliding down into the trench. "C Company o' the Stonewalls, 'e wanted."

"That's us," said Larry, "but if he wants an officer he must go higher up."

Another figure appeared on the bank above, and jumped hastily down into the trench.

"Stonewalls," he said. "Where's 'C'—why 'ere yer are, chums——"

"Pug?" said Larry and Kentucky incredulously. "We thought that— why, weren't you hit?" "Thought you was 'alf-way to Blighty by now," said Billy Simson.

"You were hit, after all," said Larry, noticing the bloodstains and the slit sleeve on Pug's jacket.

"'It?" said Billy Simson, also staring hard. "Surely they didn't send yer back 'ere after bein' casualtied?"

"Give a bloke 'alf a chance to git 'is wind," said Pug, "an' I'll spin yer the cuffer. But I'm jist about puffed out runnin' acrost that blinkin' field, and dodgin' Jack Johnsons. Thought I was niver goin' to find yer agin; bin searchin' 'alf over France since last night, tryin' to 'ook up with yer. Where've you bin to, any'ow?"

"Bin to!" said Billy Simson, indignantly. "We've bin now'ere. We've bin squatting 'ere freezin' and drownin' to death—them that 'aven't bin wiped out with crumps."

"We came straight across from where we left you to the old German trench," said Larry, "then up a communication trench to here, and, as Billy says, we've stuck here ever since."

"An' 'ere," said Pug, "I've bin trampin' miles lookin' for yer, and every man I asked w'ere the Stonewalls was told me a new plice."

"But what happened, Pug?" said Kentucky. "You were wounded, we see that; but why ar'n't you back in the dressing station?"

"Well," said Pug, hesitatingly, "w'en I got this puncture, I dropped

43

back in the trench. I didn't know w'ether it was bad or not, but one of our stretcher-bearers showed me the way back to the fust aid post. They tied me up there, and told me the wound wasn't nothin' worth worritin' about, and after a few days at the Base I'd be back to the battalion as good as ever; so I 'ad a walk round outside, waitin' till the ambulance come that they said would cart me back to the 'orspital train, and w'en nobody was lookin' I jist come away, and found my way back to w'ere yer lef' me. Then I chased round, as I've told yer, till I found yer 'ere."

"Good man," said Larry, and Kentucky nodded approvingly.

Billy Simson didn't look on it in the same light. "You 'ad a chance to go back, and you come on up 'ere agin," he said, staring hard at Pug. "For God's sake, what for?"

"Well, yer see," said Pug, "all the time I've bin out 'ere I've never 'ad a chance to see the inside of a German trench; an' now there was a fust class chance to git into one, an' a chance maybe of pickin' up a 'elmet for a soo-veneer, I thought I'd be a fool not to take it. You 'aven't none of yer found a 'elmet yet, 'ave yer?" and he looked inquiringly round.

"'Elmet," said Billy Simson disgustedly. "Blowed if yer catch me comin' back 'ere for a bloomin' 'undred 'elmets. If I'd bin you, I'd a bin snug in a 'ospital drinkin' beef tea, an' smokin' a fag by now."

"Ah!" said Pug profoundly. "But w'at good was a week at the Base to me?"

"You would 'ave missed the rest of this rotten show, any'ow," said Billy.

"That's right," assented Pug, "and I might 'ave missed my chance to pick up a 'elmet. I want a blinkin' 'elmet—see—and wot's more, I'm goin' to git one."

CHAPTER VII

BLIND MAN'S BUFF

The Sergeant stumbled round the corner of the traverse and told the four men there that the battalion was moving along the trench to the right, and to "get on and follow the next file." They rose stiffly, aching in every joint, from their cramped positions, and plodded and stumbled round the corner and along the trench. They were all a good deal amazed to see the chaotic state to which it had been reduced by the shell fire, and not only could they understand plainly now why so many casualties had been borne past them, but found it difficult to understand why the number had not been greater.

"By the state of this trench," said Larry, "you'd have thought a battalion of mice could hardly have helped being blotted out."

"It licks me," agreed Kentucky; "the whole trench seems gone to smash; but I'm afraid there must have been more casualties than came past us."

"Look out!" warned Billy Simson, "'ere's another," and the four halted and crouched again until the shell, which from the volume of sound of its coming they knew would fall near, burst in the usual thunder-clap of noise and flying débris of mud and earth. Then they rose again and moved on, and presently came to a dividing of the ways, and a sentry posted there to warn them to turn off to the left. They scrambled and floundered breathlessly along it, over portions that were choked almost to the top by fallen earth and rubble, across other parts which were no more than a shallow gutter with

45

deep shell craters blasted out of it and the ground about it. In many of these destroyed portions it was almost impossible, stoop and crouch and crawl as they would and as they did, to avoid coming into view of some part of the ground still held by the Germans, but either because the German guns were busy elsewhere, or because the whole ground was more or less veiled by the haze of smoke that drifted over it and by the thin drizzle of rain that continued to fall, the battalion escaped any concerted effort of the German guns to catch them in their scanty cover. But there were still sufficient casual shells, and more than sufficient bullets about, to make the passage of the broken trench an uncomfortable and dangerous one, and they did not know whether to be relieved or afraid when they came to a spot where an officer halted them in company with about a dozen other men, and bade them wait there until he gave the word, when they were to jump from the trench and run straight across the open to the right, about a hundred yards over to where they would find another trench, better than the one they were now occupying, then to "get down into it as quick as you can, and keep along to the left." They waited there until a further batch of men were collected, and then the officer warned them to get ready for a quick run.

"You'll see some broken-down houses over there," he said; "steer for them; the trench runs across this side of them, and you can't miss it. It's the first trench you meet; drop into it, and, remember, turn down to the left. Now—no, wait a minute."

They waited until another dropping shell had burst, and then at the quick command of the officer jumped out and ran hard in the direction of the broken walls they could just see. Most of the men ran straight without looking left or right, but Kentucky as he went glanced repeatedly to his left, towards where the German lines were. He was surprised to find that they were evidently a good way off, very much further off, in fact, than he had expected. He had thought the last communication trench up which they moved must have been bringing them very close to our forward line, but here from where he ran he could see for a clear two or three hundred yards to the first break of a trench parapet; knew that this must be in British hands, and that the German trench must lie beyond it again. He concluded that the line of captured ground must have curved forward from that part behind which they had spent the night, figured to himself that the cottages towards which they ran must be in our hands, and that the progress of the attack along there had pushed further home than they had known or expected.

46

He thought out all these things with a sort of secondary mind and consciousness. Certainly his first thoughts were very keenly on the path he had to pick over the wet ground past the honeycomb of old and new shell holes, over and through some fragments of rusty barbed wire that still clung to their broken or uptorn stakes, and his eye looked anxiously for the trench toward which they were running, and in which they would find shelter from the bullets that hissed and whisked past, or smacked noisily into the wet ground.

There was very little parapet to the trench, and the runners were upon it almost before they saw it. Billy Simson and Larry reached it first, with Pug and Kentucky close upon their heels. They wasted no time in leaping to cover, for just as they did so there came the rapid rush-rush, bang-bang of a couple of Pip-Squeak shells. The four tumbled into the trench on the instant the shells burst, but quick as they were, the shells were quicker. They heard the whistle and thump of flying fragments about them, and Billy Simson yelped as he fell, rolled over, and sat up with his hand reaching over and clutching at the back of his shoulder, his face contorted by pain.

"What is it, Billy?" said Larry quickly.

"Did it get you, son?" said Kentucky.

"They've got me," gasped Billy. "My Christ, it do 'urt."

"Lemme look," said Pug quickly. "Let's 'ave a field-dressin', one o' yer."

Simson's shoulder was already crimsoning, and the blood ran and dripped fast from it. Pug slipped out a knife, and with a couple of slashes split the torn jacket and shirt down and across.

"I don't think it's a bad 'un," he said. "Don't seem to go deep, and it's well up on the shoulder anyway."

"It's bad enough," said Billy, "by the way it 'urts."

Kentucky also examined the wound closely.

"I'm sure Pug's right," he said. "It isn't anyways dangerous, Billy."

Billy looked up suddenly. "It's a Blighty one, isn't it?" he said anxiously.

"Oh, yes," said Kentucky; "a Blighty one, sure."

"Good enough," said Billy Simson. "If it's a Blighty one I've got plenty. I'm not like you, Pug; I'm not thirstin' enough for Germ 'elmets to go lookin' any further for 'em."

One of the sergeants came pushing along the trench, urging the men to get a move on and clear out before the next lot ran across the open for the shelter.

"Man wounded," he said, when they told him of Billy Simson. "You, Simson! Well, you must wait 'ere, and I'll send a stretcher-bearer back, if ye're not able to foot it on your own."

"I don't feel much up to footin' it," said Billy Simson. "I think I'll stick here until somebody comes to give me a hand."

So the matter was decided, and the rest pushed along the narrow trench, leaving Simson squatted in one of the bays cut out of the wall. The others moved slowly along to where their trench opened into another running across it, turned down this, and went wandering along its twisting, curving loops until they had completely lost all sense of direction.

The guns on both sides were maintaining a constant cannonade, and the air overhead shook continually to the rumble and wail and howl of the passing shells. But although it was difficult to keep a sense of direction, there was one thing always which told them how they moved—the rattle of rifle fire, the rapid rat-tat-tatting of the machine guns and sharp explosions of bombs and grenades. These sounds, as they all well knew, came from the fighting front, from the most advanced line where our men still strove to push forward, and the enemy stood to stay them, or to press them back.

The sound kept growing ominously louder and nearer the further the Stonewalls pushed on along their narrow trench, and now they could hear, even above the uproar of the guns and of the firing lines, the sharp hiss and zipp of the bullets passing close above the trench, the hard smacks and cracks with which they struck the parapet or the ground about it. The trench in which they moved was narrow, deep, and steep-sided. It was therefore safe from everything except the direct overhead burst of high-explosive shrapnel, and of these there were, for the moment, few or none; so that when the men were halted and kept waiting for half an hour they could see nothing except the narrow strip of sky above the lips of the trench, but could at least congratulate themselves that they were out of the inferno in which they had spent the night and the early part of the morning. It was still raining, a thin, cold, drizzling rain, which collected in the trench bottom and turned the path into gluey mud, trickled down the walls and saturated them to a sticky clay which daubed the shoulders, the elbows, the hips, and haversacks of the men as they pushed along, coated them with a layer of clinging, slimy wetness, clammy to the touch, and striking them through and through with shivering chills. When they halted most of the men squatted down in the bottom of the trench, sitting on their heels and leaning their backs against the walls, and waited there, listening to the near-by uproar of the conflict, speculating on how little or how long a time it would be before they were into it actively; discussing and guessing at the progress the attack had made, and what ground had been taken, and held or lost. Here and there a man spoke of this point or that which the attack had reached, of some village or hill, or trench, which he heard had been taken. Usually the information had been gleaned from wounded men, from the stretcher-bearers and ammunition carriers with whom the Stonewalls had spoken, as they crossed and recrossed their trench early that morning.

In the trench they now occupied they gleaned no further news, because none of these wayfarers to and from the firing-line passed their way.

"Our front line can't be getting pushed very hard," suggested Larry; "because if they were, they'd have shoved us in support before now."

"It looks to me," said Kentucky, "that they have slid us off quite a piece to the right of where we were meant to go. What lot of ours do you suppose is in these trenches in front of us now?" But of that nobody had any definite opinion, although several made guesses, based on the vaguest rumors, and knowledge of this regiment or that which had gone up ahead of them.

"'Ark at the Archies," said Pug suddenly. "They're 'avin' a busy season on somebody. D'yer think they're ours, or the 'Uns'?"

"I don't know," said Kentucky, "but I fancy I hear the 'planes they're shooting at."

He was right, and presently they all heard the faint but penetrating whirr of an aeroplane's engines, even above the louder and deeper note of the cannonade and rifle fire.

"There she is," said Larry. "Can you see the marks on her?"

"It's ours," said Kentucky. "I see the rings plain enough."

Although the aeroplane was at a good height, there were several who could distinguish the bull's-eye target pattern of the red, white and blue circles painted on the wings and marking the aeroplane as British. For some time it pursued a course roughly parallel to the line of the trench, so that the Stonewalls, craning their heads back, could follow its progress along the sky, and the trailing wake of puffing smoke from the shrapnel that followed it. They lost sight of it presently until it curved back into the range of their vision, and came sailing swiftly over them again. Then another 'plane shot into view above them, steering straight for the first, and with a buzz of excited comment the Stonewalls proclaimed it a Hun and speculated keenly on the chances of a "scrap."

There was a "scrap," and in its opening phases the Stonewalls had an excellent view of the two machines circling, swooping, soaring, and diving in graceful, bird-like curves. The "Archies" ceased on both sides to fling their shrapnel at the airy opponents, because with their swift dartings to and fro, and still more because of their proximity to one another, the Archie gunners were just as liable to wing their own 'plane and bring it down, as they were to hit the enemy one. For two or three minutes the Stonewalls watched with the wildest excitement and keenest interest the maneuvering of the two machines. Half a dozen times a gasp or a groan, or a chorus of comment "He's hit," and "He's downed," and "He's got him," followed some movement, some daring plunge or nose dive of one or other of the machines; but always before the exclamations had finished the supposed injured one had righted itself, swooped and soared upward again, and swung circling into its opponent.

Once or twice the watchers thought they could catch the faint far-off rattle of the aeroplanes' machine guns, although amongst the other sounds of battle it was difficult to say with any certainty that these shots were fired in the air; but just when the interest and excitement were at their highest, a sharp order was passed along the trench for every man to keep his face down, on no account to look upwards out of the trench, and officers and sergeants, very reluctantly setting the good example by stooping their own heads, pushed along the trench to see that the men also obeyed the order.

"Blinkin' sell, I calls it," exclaimed Pug disgustedly. "The fust decent scrap between two 'planes I've ever 'ad a chance to see, and 'ere I'm not allowed to look at it."

"You wait until you get 'ome, and see it on the pictures," said the Sergeant, who stood near them. "It'll be a sight safer there. If you don't know you ought to, that a trench full of white faces lookin' up at a 'plane, is as good as sending a postcard to their spotter upstairs sayin' the trench is occupied in force; and I don't suppose," he concluded, "you're any more anxious than I am for that 'Un to be sendin' a wireless to his guns, and 'avin' this trench strafed like the last one was."

"From what I can see of it," said Pug, "that 'Un up there was 'avin' 'is 'ands too full to worrit about wot was goin' on down 'ere."

"Well, anyhow," said the Sergeant, "you needn't keep yer eyes down lookin' for sixpences any longer. Both the 'planes is out of sight."

"Well, I'm blowed," said Pug, "if that's not a sickener. 'Ere we 'as a fust-class fight, and us in the front seats for seein' it, and they goes and shifts off so we don't even know which side won."

And they never did. A minute later the anti-aircraft guns broke out into fire again, their peculiar singing reports easily distinguishable from the other gun fire, even as the distant reports of their shrapnel bursts in the air were distinguishable from the other sounds of many bursting shells near the ground. But which of the "Archibalds" were firing they did not know. They could only guess that one of the machines had been shot down, and that the anti-aircraft guns of the opposing side were endeavoring to bring down the victor—but which was the victor, and whether he escaped or not, was never known to the Stonewalls.

"Bloomin' Blind-Man's-Buff, I calls it," grumbled Pug. "Gropin' round after 'Uns you can't see, an' gettin' poked in the ribs without seein' one—like Billy was."

51

CHAPTER VIII

OVER THE TOP

The long-delayed and long-expected crisis in the affairs of the Stonewalls came at last about midday, and they were moved up into the front line, into the battered trench held by the remains of another battalion.

This line ran curving and zigzagging some fifty to a hundred yards beyond the shattered and shell-smitten fragments of a group of houses which stood on the grass-and weed-grown remains of a road. What was now the British front line of trench had been at one time a German communication trench in part of its length, and apparently some sort of support trench in another part. But throughout its whole length it had been so battered and wrecked, rent and riven asunder by shell fire, by light and heavy bombs of every sort and description, that it was all of much the same pattern—a comparatively wide ditch, filled up and choked to half its depth in some places by fallen walls and scattered sandbags, in other parts no more than a line of big and little shell-craters linked up by a shallow ditch, with a tangle of barbed wire flung out in coils and loops in front of the trench, with here and there a few strands run out and staked down during the night.

The face of the trench was no longer a perpendicular wall with a proper fire step, as all regularly constructed trenches are made when possible; the walls had crumbled down under the explosions of shell and bomb, and although some attempt had been made to improve the defenses, actually these improvements had been of the

52

slightest description, and in many cases were destroyed again as fast as they were made; so for the most part the men of the battalion holding the trench picked little angles and corners individually for themselves, did their best to pile sandbags for head cover, lay sprawling on or against the sloping trench wall, and fired over the parapet.

At the point occupied by the Stonewalls the opposing lines were too far apart for the throwing of hand grenades, but the line was still suffering a fairly heavy and uncomfortably accurate artillery bombardment. The trench was strewn along its length with a débris of torn sandbags, of packs and equipments stripped from the wounded, of rifles and bayonets, mess-tins, and trenching tools, and caps and boots and water-bottles. Collected here and there in odd corners were many dead, because scattered along the whole length of line there were still many wounded, and until these had been safely removed there could, of course, be no time or consideration spared for attention to the dead.

The Stonewalls passed in single file along the broken trench behind the men who still held the position and lay and fired over their parapet. There were many remarks from these men, caustic inquiries as to where the Stonewalls had been, and why they had taken so long to come up; expressions of relief that they had come; inquiries as to whether there was to be another attack, or whether they were to be relieved by the Stonewalls, and allowed to go back. The Stonewalls, of course, could give no information as to what would happen, because of that they themselves had not the faintest idea. They were pushed along the trench and halted in a much closer and stronger line than the widely spaced men of the defending force which had held it.

Larry remarked on this to Pug and Kentucky, when at last the little group of which they were a part was told by their Sergeant to halt.

"I suppose," said Kentucky, "we're thicker along this line because there's more of us. Whether the same reason will hold good by this time to-morrow is another proposition."

"I'm goin' to 'ave a peep out," said Pug, and scrambled up the sloping face of the trench to beside a man lying there.

"Hello, chum!" said this man, turning his head to look at Pug. "Welcome to our 'ome, as the text says, and you'll be a bloomin'

53

sight more welcome if you're takin' over, and lettin' us go back. I've 'ad quite enough of this picnic for one turn."

"'As it bin pretty 'ot here?" asked Pug.

The man slid his rifle-barrel over a sandbag, raised his head and took hasty aim, fired, and ducked quickly down again. "'Ot!" he repeated. "I tell yer 'ell's a bloomin' ice cream barrow compared to wot this trench 'as been since we come in it. 'Ot? My blanky oath!"

Pug raised his head cautiously, and peered out over the parapet.

"I s'pose that's their trench acrost there," he said doubtfully, "but it's a rummy lookin' mix up. Wot range are yer shootin' at?"

"Pretty well point blank," said the private. "It's about 200 to 250 they tell me."

"'Oo's trench is that along there to the left?" asked Pug. "It seems to run both ways."

"I'm not sure," said the other man, "but I expect it's an old communication trench. This bit opposite us they reckon is a kind of redoubt; you'll notice it sticks out to a point that their trenches slope back from on both sides."

"I notice there's a 'eap of wire all round it," said Pug, and bobbed his head down hastily at the whizz of a couple of bullets. "And that's blinkin' well enough to notice," he continued, "until I 'as to look out an' notice some more whether I likes it or not."

He slipped down again into the trench bottom, and described such of the situation as he had seen, as well as he could. He found the others discussing a new rumor, which had just arrived by way of the Sergeant. The tale ran that they were to attack the trenches opposite; that there was to be an intense artillery bombardment first, that the assault was to be launched after an hour or two of this.

"I 'ear there's a battalion of the Jocks joined up to our left in this trench," said the Sergeant, "and there's some Fusilier crowd packin' in on our right."

"That looks like business," said Larry; "but is it true, do you think, Sergeant? Where did you get it from?"

"There's a 'tillery forward officer a little piece along the trench there,

54

and I was 'avin' a chat with 'is signaler. They told me about the attack, and told me their Battery was goin' to cut the wire out in front of us."

Kentucky, who was always full of curiosity and interest in unusual proceedings, decided to go along and see the Forward Officer at work. He told the others he would be back in a few minutes, and, scrambling along the trench, found the Artillery Subaltern and two signalers. The signalers had a portable telephone connected up with the trailing wire, and over this the Subaltern was talking when Kentucky arrived. He handed the receiver to one of his signalers, and crossing the trench took up a position where by raising his head he could see over the parapet.

"Number One gun, fire," he said, and the signaler repeated the words over the telephone, and a moment later called sharply: "No. 1 fired, sir."

Kentucky waited expectantly with his eye on the Forward Officer, waited so many long seconds for any sound of the arriving shell or any sign of the Officer's movement that he was beginning to think he had misunderstood the method by which the game was played; but at that moment he heard a sudden and savage rush of air close overhead, saw the Forward Officer straighten up and stare anxiously out over the parapet, heard the sharp crash of the bursting shell out in front. The Officer stooped his head again and called something about dropping twenty-five and repeating. The signaler gave his message word for word over the 'phone, and a minute later reported again: "No. 1 fired, sir."

Kentucky, not knowing the technicalities of gunners' lingo, was unable to follow the meaning of the orders as they were passed back from the officer to the signaler, from the signaler to the Battery. There was talk of adding and dropping, of so many minutes right or left, of lengthening and shortening, and of "correctors"; but although he could not understand all this, the message was clear enough when the officer remarked briefly:

"Target No. 1; register that," and proceeded to call for No. 2 gun, and to repeat the complicated directions of ranges and deflection. Presently No. 2 found its target also, and the Forward Officer went on with three and the remaining guns in turn. For the first few shots from each he stood up to look over the parapet, but after that viewed the proceedings through a periscope.

Kentucky, establishing himself near the signaler, who was for the moment disengaged, talked with him, and acquired some of the simpler mysteries of registering a target, and of wire cutting. "He stands up at first," explained the signaler, in answer to an inquiry, "because he pitches the first shell well over to be on the safe side. He has to catch the burst as soon as it goes, and he mightn't have his periscope aimed at the right spot. After he corrects the lay, and knows just where the round is going to land, he can keep his periscope looking there and waiting for it. It's not such a risky game then, but we gets a heap of F.O.O.'s casualtied doing those first peeps over the parapet."

After the Forward Officer had got all his guns correctly laid, the Battery opened a rapid and sustained fire, and the shells, pouring in a rushing stream so close over the trench that the wind of their passing could be felt, burst in a running series of reports out in front.

Kentucky made his way back to his own portion of the trench, and borrowing a pocket looking-glass periscope, clipped it to his bayonet and watched for some time with absorbed interest the tongues of flame that licked out from the bursting shells, and the puffing clouds of smoke that rolled along the ground in front of the German parapet. The destruction of the wire was plain to see, and easy to watch. The shells burst one after another over and amongst it, and against the background of smoke that drifted over the ground the tangle of wire stood up clearly, and could be seen dissolving and vanishing under the streams of shrapnel bullets. As time passed the thick hedge of wire that had been there at first was broken down and torn away; the stakes that held it were knocked down or splintered to pieces or torn up and flung whirling from the shell bursts. Other batteries had come into play along the same stretch of front, and were hard at work destroying in the same fashion the obstacle to the advance of the infantry. The meaning of the wire cutting must have been perfectly plain to the Germans; clearly it signified an attack; clearly that signified the forward trenches being filled with a strong attacking force; and clearly again that meant a good target for the German guns, a target upon which they proceeded to play with savage intensity.

The forward and support lines were subjected to a tornado of high explosive and shrapnel fire, and again the Stonewalls were driven to crouching in their trench while the big shells pounded down, round, and over and amongst them. They were all very sick of these repeated series of hammerings from the German guns, and Pug voiced the idea of a good many, when at the end of a couple of hours the message came along that they were to attack with the bayonet in fifteen minutes.

"I don't s'pose the attack will be any picnic," he said, "but blow me if I wouldn't rather be up there with a chance of gettin' my own back, than stickin' in this stinkin' trench and gettin' blown to sausage meat without a chance of crookin' my finger to save myself."

For two hours past the British guns had been giving as good as they were getting, and a little bit better to boot; but now for the fifteen minutes previous to the assault their fire worked up to a rate and intensity that must have been positively appalling to the German defenders of the ground opposite, and especially of the point which was supposed to be a redoubt. The air shook to the rumble and yell and roar of the heavy shells, vibrated to the quicker and closer rush of the field guns' shrapnel. The artillery fire for the time being dominated the field, and brought the rifle fire from the opposing trenches practically to silence, so that it was possible with some degree of safety for the Stonewalls to look over their parapet and watch with a mixture of awe and delight the spectacle of leaping whirlwinds of fire and billowing smoke, the spouting débris that splashed upwards, through them; to listen to the deep rolling detonations and shattering boom of the heavy shells that poured without ceasing on the trenches in front of them.

"If there's any bloomin' Germans left on that ground," said Pug cheerfully, "I'd like to know 'ow they do it. Seems to me a perishin' black-beetle in a 'ole could not 'ave come through that shell fire if 'e 'ad as many lives as a cat."

It almost looked as if he was right, and that the defense had been obliterated by the artillery preparation, for when the order came along and the British Infantry began to scramble hurriedly over the parapet, to make their way out through the wire, and to form up quickly and roughly on the open ground beyond it, hardly a shot was fired at them, and there was no sound or sign of life in the German trenches except the whirling smoke clouds starred with quick flashes of fire from the shells that still streamed overhead and battered and hammered down on the opposite lines.

The infantry lay down in the wet grass and mud for another two or three minutes, and then, suddenly and simultaneously, as if all the guns had worked together on the pulling of a string, the shells, without ceasing for an instant to roar past overhead, ceased to flame and crash on the forward lines, but began to pound down in a belt of smoke and fire some hundreds of yards beyond. Along the length of the British line whistle after whistle trilled and shrieked; a few figures could be seen leaping to their feet and beginning to run forward; and then with a heave and a jumble of bobbing heads and shoulders the whole line rose and swung forward in a long, uneven, but almost solid wave. At the same instant the German trenches came to life, a ragged volley of rifle fire crackled out, grew closer and quicker, swelled into one tumultuous roll with the machine guns hammering and rapping and clattering sharply and distinctly through the uproar. About the ears of the running infantry could be heard the sharp hiss and zipp and whistle and whine of passing bullets; from the ground amongst their feet came the cracking and snapping of bullets striking and the spurts of mud thrown up by them. At first these sounds were insignificant, and hardly noticed in the greater and more terrifying clamor of the guns' reports, the shriek and whoop of the passing shells, the crashing bursts of their explosions. But the meaning and significance of the hissing bullet sounds were made swiftly plain as the rifle and machine-gun fire grew, and the riflemen and machine gunners steadied to their aim and task. The bullet storm swept down on the charging line, and the line withered and melted and shredded away under it. It still advanced steadily, but the ground behind it was dotted thicker and closer and more and more quickly with the bodies of men who fell and lay still, or crawled back towards their parapet or to the shelter of the nearest shell crater. The line went on, but half-way across the open ground it began to show ragged and uneven with great gaps sliced out of it at intervals. The wet ground was heavy going, and the fierceness of the fire and the numbers struck down by it began to make it look a doubtful question whether a sufficient weight of men could reach their goal to carry the charge home with any effect. From one cause or another the pace slowed sensibly, although the men themselves were probably unaware of the slowing.

Kentucky, Larry, and Pug kept throughout within arm's length of one another. They had set out under the same bargain to keep close and help one another if need arose; but Kentucky at least confesses that any thoughts of a bargain, any memory of an arranged program, had completely left him, and very probably his thoughts ran in much the same direction as three-fourths of the charging line.

His whole mind, without any conscious effort of reasoning, was centered on getting over the open as quickly as possible, of coming to hand grips with the Germans, of getting down into their trench out of reach of the sleeting bullets that swept the open. He arrived at the conclusion that in the open he was no more than a mere helpless running target for shells and bullets; that once in the German trench he would be out of reach of these; that if the trench were held and it came to hand-to-hand fighting, at least he would stand an equal chance, and at least his hand could guard his head. How many men he might have to meet, what odds would be against him, whether the attackers would be thinned out to a hopeless outnumbering, he hardly troubled to think. That need could be met as it arose, and in the meantime the first and more imperative need was to get across the open, to escape the bullets that pelted about them. He ran on quite unconscious of whether the rest of the line was still advancing, or whether it had been exterminated. Arrived at the wrecked entanglements of wire he did look round, to find Larry and Pug close beside him, and all three plunged into the remains of the entanglement almost side by side, and began to kick and tear a way over and through the remaining strands and the little chopped fragments that strewed the ground.

Kentucky was suddenly aware of a machine-gun embrasure almost in front of them, placed in an angle of the trench so as to sweep the open ground in enfilade. From the blackness of the embrasure mouth flashed a spitting stream of fire, and it came to him with a jerk that on the path he was taking he would have to cross that stream, that the bullets pouring from it must inevitably cut down his two companions and himself. He turned and shouted hoarsely at them, swerved to one side, and slanted in to the trench so as to escape the streaming fire; but, looking round, he saw that the other two had not heard or heeded him, that they were still plowing straight on through the broken wires, that another few paces must bring them directly in the path of the bullets' sweep. He yelled again hoarsely, but realized as he did so that his voice was lost and drowned in the clamor of the battle. But at that instant—and this was the first instant that he became aware of others beside the three of them having come so far—a man plunged past him, halted abruptly, and hurled something straight at the black hole of the embrasure. The bomb went true to its mark, the embrasure flamed out a broad gush of fire, a loud report boomed thunderously and hollowly from it—and the spitting fire stream stopped abruptly.

59

Kentucky ran on, leaped at the low parapet, scrambled on top of it, swung the point of his bayonet down, and poised himself for the leap. Below him he saw three faces staring upward, three rifle muzzles swing towards him and hang, as it seemed, for an eternity pointed straight at his face.

His mind was so full of that overpowering thought it had carried all the way across the open, the desperate desire to get down into the trench, that, confronted by the rifle muzzles and the urgent need to do something to escape them, he could not for the moment readjust his thoughts or rearrange his actions. The instant's hesitation might easily have been fatal, and it is probable he owed his life to another man who at that moment leaped on the broken parapet and jostled him roughly just as two of the rifles below flamed and banged. As he half reeled aside from that jolting elbow he felt a puff of wind in his face, was conscious of a tremendous blow and violent upward leaping sensation somewhere about his head, a rush of cold air on his scalp. His first foolish thought was that the top of his head had been blown away, and he half dropped to his knees, clutching with one hand at his bare head, from which the shot had whirled his helmet. And as he dropped he saw beside him on the parapet the man who had jostled him, saw the swift downward fling of his hand as he hurled something into the trench and instantly flung himself to ground. Kentucky realized what the bomber was doing just in time to duck backwards. A yell from the trench below was cut short by a crashing report, a spout of flame and smoke shot up, and the parapet trembled and shuddered. The bomber leaped to his feet and without a word to Kentucky leaped across the trench and ran along its further side, swinging another bomb by its stick-handle. He carried a lot more of these hanging and dangling about his body. They jerked as he ran, and it flashed across Kentucky's mind to wonder if there was no possibility of two of them by some mischance striking and detonating one another, or the safety pins jolting out, when he saw the man crumple suddenly and fall sprawling and lie still where he fell. Reminded abruptly of his exposed position and of those significant whiskings and swishings through the air about him, Kentucky jumped to his feet, glanced over into the trench, and jumped down into it. At the moment he could see no other British soldier to either side of him, but in the trench bottom lay the three bodies of the men killed by the bomb. A sudden wild and nervous doubt shot into his mind—could he be the only man who had safely reached the trench? But on the same instant he heard cries, the rush of feet, and two or three men leaped

60

over and down into the trench beside him, and he caught a glimpse of others doing the same further along.

"Seen any of 'em?" gasped one of the newcomers, and without waiting an answer, "Come along, men; work along the trench and look out for dug-outs."

Kentucky recognized them as men of another company of the Stonewalls, saw that they, too, were loaded with bombs, and because he was not at all sure what he ought to do himself, he followed them along the trench. The bombers stopped at the dark entrance to a dug-out, and the officer leading them halted and shouted down it. In reply a rifle banged and a bullet hissed out past the officer's head. The men swore, stepped hurriedly aside, and one of them swung forward a bomb with long cloth streamers dangling from it. "Not that," said the officer quickly. "It'll explode on the stairs. Give 'em two or three Mills' grenades." The men pulled the pins from the grenades and flung them down the stairway and the rifle banged angrily again. "That's about your last shot," said one of the men grimly, and next instant a hollow triple report boomed out from deep below. "Roll another couple down to make sure," said the officer, "and come along."

Kentucky remembered the episode of the double entrance to the dug-out in the other trench. "There may be another stair entrance further along," he said quickly. "Come on," said the officer abruptly, "we'll see. You'd better come with us and have your bayonet ready. I've lost my bayonet men." He led the way himself with a long "trench dagger" in his hand—a murderous looking long knife with rings set along the haft for his fingers to thrust through and grip. Kentucky heard a shout of "C Company. Rally along here, C."

"I'd better go, hadn't I?" he asked. "I'm C, and they're shouting for C."

"All right," said the officer, "push off. Pick up that rifle, one of you. It's a German, but it'll do for bayonet work if we need it."

Kentucky had no idea where "C" Company was calling from, and down in the trench he could see nothing. For a moment he was half inclined to stay where he was with the others, but the shout came again, "C Company. Along here, C." He scrambled up the broken rear wall of the trench, saw a group of men gathering along to the right, heard another call from them, and climbed out to run stooping across and join them.

61

"Hello, Kentucky," he heard, "where you bin? Thought you was a wash-out."

"I'm all hunkadory, Pug," he answered joyfully. "I missed you coming across just after that bomber slung one in on the machine gun. Lucky thing for you he did, too."

"Hey?" said Pug vaguely, "wot bomber, an' wot machine gun?"

"Well, I didn't think you could have missed seeing that," said Kentucky in astonishment. "You and Larry were running right across its muzzle. But where's Larry?"

"Dunno," said Pug anxiously. "I thought 'im an' you would be together. He was with me not more'n a minute or two afore we got in. Hope 'e 'asn't been an' stopped one."

"Do you remember where you got in?" said Kentucky. "I believe I could find where that machine gun was. If he was hit it must have been there or in the trench here. I think we ought to go and hunt for him."

But their officer and sergeant had other and more imperative ideas as to their immediate program. "Pick up any of those picks and spades you see lying about," ordered the sergeant, "and try'n get this trench into shape a bit. The rest of you get on to those sandbags and pile 'em up for a parapet. Sharp, now, every man there. You, Pug, get along with it, bear a hand. That arm of yours all right? If it isn't you'd best shove along back to the rear."

CHAPTER IX

A SIDE SHOW

Although Pug and Kentucky were not allowed to go and look for their lost chum, and in fact did not know for long enough what had happened to him, the tale of that happening, I think, fits best in here. It is perhaps all the more worth the telling because it is a sample of scores of incidents that may never be heard of outside the few who participated in them, but are characteristic of one of the most amazing features of the New Armies—and that, mark you, is rather a big word, remembering we are speaking of something which itself is nothing but one huge amazing feature—the readiness and smoothness with which it has fallen into professional soldiering ways and the instinct for fighting which over and over again it has been proved to possess. And by fighting instinct I do not mean so much that animal instinct which every man has hidden somewhere in his make-up to look out for himself and kill the fellow who is trying to kill him, but rather that peculiar instinct which picks a certain corner of a trench as a key to a local position, which knows that if a certain bit of ground can be taken or held it will show much more than its face value, which senses the proper time to hang on and the right moment to risk a rush.

These, of course, are the instincts of leadership, and these are the instincts which the New Army has shown it possesses, not only in its officers and non-coms., but time and again—in innumerable little-known or unknown incidents of battle that have been lost in the bigger issues—in the rank and file, in privates who never were taught or expected to know anything about leadership, in men brought up to every possible trade, profession and occupation except war. One can only suppose it is an instinct deep rooted in the race that has lain dormant for generations, and only come to life again in the reviving heat of war.

It will be remembered that Larry became separated from his two friends in their rush on the German line, and just as they reached the remains of the barbed wire before the German trench. For the greater part the wire had been uprooted and swept away by the storm of British shells and mortar bombs, but here and there it still remained sufficiently intact to make a difficult and unpleasant obstacle.

Larry and Pug, deflected from their course by one or two yawning shell craters, ran into one of these undestroyed patches of wire, and while Pug turned to the left, Larry turned right and ran skirting along its edge in search of a place through. Several other men did the same, and by the time they had found an opening there were about a score of them to go streaming through the gap and plunging at the broken parapet. Half of them were shot down in that last dozen yards, and as they opened out and went clawing and scrambling at the parapet with rifles banging almost in their faces, hand grenades lobbed over to roll down amongst their feet and explode in showers of flying splinters. The few who for the moment escaped these dangers, knowing that every instant they remained in the open outside the trench carried almost a certainty of sudden death, flung desperately at its parapet, over and down into it among the German bayonets, without stopping to count or heed what the hand-to-hand odds might be.

Larry Arundel, at the lip of the trench, suddenly finding himself poised above a group of some four or five men, checked his downward leap from a first instinctive and absurd fear of hurting the men he would jump down upon, recovered himself, and swung his rifle forward and thrust and again thrust savagely down at the gray coats and helmets below him, saw the bright steel strike and pierce a full half its length with no other feeling than a faint surprise that he should sense so little check to its smooth swing, shortened the grip on his rifle, and, thrusting again as he jumped, leaped down into the space his bayonet had cleared. The last man he had stabbed at evaded the thrust, and like a flash stabbed back as Larry landed in the trench. But the two were too close for the point to be effective, and Larry's hip and elbow turned the weapon aside. He found himself almost breast to breast with his enemy, and partly because there was no room to swing a bayonet, partly because that undefended face and point of the jaw awoke the boxer's instinct, his clenched fist jerked in a fierce uppercut hard and true to its mark, and the German grunted once and dropped as if pole-axed.

But there Larry's career would probably have cut short, because there were still a couple of men within arm's length of him, and both were on the point of attacking, when another little batch of belated attackers arrived at the trench. Several of them struck in at the point where Larry was engaged with his opponents, and that particular scrimmage terminated with some abruptness.

Larry was a little dazed with the speed at which events of the past minute had happened and also to some extent by the rather stunning report of a rifle fired just past his ear by a somewhat hasty rescuer in settlement of the account of his nearest opponent.

"Wh-what's happened?" he asked. "Have we got this trench all right?"

"Looks like it," said one of the others. "But blest if I know how much of it. There didn't seem to be much of our line get in along to the right there to take their bit of front."

"Let's have a look," said Larry, and scrambled up the broken side of the trench. He stood there a minute until half a dozen bullets whistling and zipping close past sent him ducking fast to cover.

"They've got the trench to our right safe enough," he said, "and they seem to be advancing beyond it. I suppose we ought to go on, too."

"Wot's this fakement?" asked one of the men who had been poking round amongst the débris of the shattered trench. He held out a two-armed affair with glasses at the ends.

"That," said Larry quickly, taking it and raising it above the edge of the trench—"that's some sort of a periscope." He looked out through it a moment and added: "And a dash good one it is, too.... I say, that line of ours advancing on the right is getting it in the neck.... Machine-gun fire it looks like.... They've stopped.... Most of 'em are down, and the rest running back to the trench."

He was interrupted by an exclamation from one of the other men who had climbed up to look over the edge.

"Look out," he said hurriedly. "Bomb over," and he dropped back quickly into the trench.

A German stick grenade sailed over, fell on the trench parapet above them, rolled a little, and lay still, and in another second or two went off with a crash, half deafening and blinding them with the noise and smoke, but hurting no one. Some of the men swore, and one demanded angrily where the thing had come from, and "Who frew dat brick?" quoted another.

But there was little room for jests. One, two, three grenades came over in quick succession; one going over and missing the trench, another falling in it at the toe of a man who promptly and neatly kicked it clear round the corner of the traverse, where it exploded harmlessly; but the third falling fairly in the trench, where it burst, just as a man grabbed for it to throw it out, killing him instantly and slightly wounding one or two others.

"Who's got those Mills?" said Larry hurriedly. "You, Harvey—chuck a couple over the traverse to the right. Must be some of them in there."

Harvey drew the pins out of a couple of Mills' grenades and tossed them over, but even as they burst another couple of German grenades came over, one bursting in the air and the other failing to explode.

"I've spotted them," suddenly said Larry, who had been watching out through the periscope. "There's some sort of trench running into this about a dozen yards along. They're in there; I saw the grenades come over out of it."

Some of the men with him had moved back out of section of trench under bombardment, and as more grenades began to lob over there was a mild stampede of the others round the traverse. Larry went with them, but pulled up at the corner and spoke sharply.

"See here, it's no good letting them chase us out like this. They'll only follow up and bomb us out traverse by traverse till there's none of us left to bomb out. Let's have some of those grenades, Harvey, and we'll rush them out of it."

Some of the men hesitated, and others demurred, muttering that there weren't enough of them, didn't know how many Germs there were, ought to find an officer and let him know.

66

It was just here that Larry took hold and saved what might have been an ugly situation. He saw instinctively what their temporary or partial retirement might mean. The advance on the right had been held up, had evidently secured that portion of the trench, but could only be holding it weakly. The trench from which the grenades had come was evidently a communicating trench. If the Germans were free to push down it in force they might re-secure a footing in the captured main trench, and there would be no knowing at what cost of time and men it would have to be retaken from them.

All this he saw, and he also saw the need for prompt action. No officer, no non-commissioned officer even, was with them, and by the time they had sent back word of the position the Germans might have secured their footing. Apparently there was no one else there willing or able to take command, so Larry took it.

He had never given a real order in his life—even his orders to the office boy or typist at home had always been in the form of "Will you please?" or "Do you mind?" He had no actual authority now to give commands, was the junior in years and in service to several there. But give orders he did, and, moreover, he gave them so clear and clean-cut, and with such an apparent conviction that they would be obeyed, that actually they were obeyed just as unhesitatingly and willingly as if he had been Colonel of the regiment.

In three minutes his dispositions were made and his directions given, in four minutes his little attack had been launched, in five minutes or little more it had succeeded, and he was "in possession of the objective." He had about half a score of men with him and a very limited supply of grenades, obviously not sufficient strength to attempt a deliberate bombing fight along the trench. So at the greater risk perhaps, but with a greater neck-or-nothing chance of success, he decided to lead his little party with a rush out of the trench across the angle of the ground to where he had seen the branching trench running into theirs.

Two men were told off to jump out on the side they had entered, to run along under cover of the parapet and shoot at any one who emerged or showed in the entrance to the communication trench; two more to fling over a couple of grenades into the trench section into which the communication-way entered and follow it up with their bayonets ready, one to push on along the trench and bring any assistance he could raise, the other to be joined by the two men above, and, if the main attack succeeded, to push up along the communication-way and join Larry's party.

This left Larry with half-a-dozen men to lead in his rush over the open. The whole of his little plans worked out neatly, exactly, and rapidly. He waited for the crash of the two grenades his bombers flung, then at his word "Go!" the two men told off heaved themselves over the rear parapet, and in a few seconds were pelting bullets down the communication trench entrance; the bombers scuffled along the trench without meeting any resistance.

Larry and his men swarmed up and out from their cover, charged across the short, open space, and in a moment were running along the edge of the communication trench, shooting and stabbing and tossing down grenades into it on top of the surprised Germans there. There were about a score of these clustered mainly near the juncture with the other trench, and in half a minute this little spot was converted into a reeking shambles under the bursting grenades and the bullets that poured into it from the two enfilading rifles.

Every man in that portion of trench was killed—one might almost say butchered—without a chance of resistance. Another string of Germans apparently being hurried along the trench as re-enforcements, were evidently stampeded by the uproar of crashing bombs and banging rifles, the yells and shouts of the attackers.

They turned and bolted back along their trench, Larry's men in the open above them pursuing and slaughtering them without mercy, until suddenly, somewhere across the open, some rifles and a machine gun began to sweep the open, and a storm of bullets to hail and patter about the little party of Stonewalls.

Larry promptly ordered them down into the trench, and they leaped in, and, under cover from the bullets above, continued to push the retreating Germans for another hundred yards along the trench.

Here the enemy made a determined stand, and Larry instantly realized that, with his weak force, he had pushed his attack to the limit of safety. He left a couple of men there to keep the enemy in clay for a few minutes with a show of pressing the attack with persistent bombing, and hurried the others back to a point that offered the best chance of making a stand.

He chose a short, straight stretch of trench running into a wide and deep pit blown out by one of our heavy shells. Round the edge of this shell-crater pit ran a ready-made parapet thrown up by the explosion, and forming a barricade across the two points where the trench ran in and out of it.

Man by man, Larry pointed out to his little force the spot each was to occupy, and bade him dig in for his life to make cover against the bombing that would assuredly be their portion very soon. He himself crawled up on to the open to some uprooted barbed wire he had noticed, was dragging together all the tangled strands and stakes he could move, when he noticed a rusty reel of wire, half unwound, grabbed that, and shuffled back into the trench.

A shrill whistle brought his two outposts hurrying and hobbling in, one of them wounded in the leg by a grenade fragment, the other with a clean bullet wound through his forearm.

The barbed wire was hastily unreeled and piled in loose coils and loops and tangles in the straight bit of trench through which the Germans must come at the pit, while from the pit barricade one man tossed a grenade at intervals over the heads of the workers into the section of trench beyond them. But the wiring job had to be left incomplete when the arrival of two or three grenades gave warning of the coming attack, and Larry and the others scrambled hurriedly over the barricade parapet into the pit.

For the next ten minutes a hot fight—small in point of the numbers engaged and space covered, but savage in its intensity and speed—raged round the pit. The Germans tried first to force their way through by sheer weight of bombing. But the Stonewalls had made full use of their trenching tools and any scattered sandbags they could pick up, and had made very good cover for themselves. Each man was dug into a niche round the inside of the parapet from which he could look out either over the open ground or back into the pit.

The Germans showered grenades over into the wired trench and the pit, and followed their explosions with a rush for the barricade. Larry, with one man to either side of him, behind the pit rim where it blocked the trench, stopped the rush with half-a-dozen well-placed Mills' grenades.

Almost at once the enemy copied the Stonewalls' first plan of attack, and, climbing suddenly from their trench, made to run along the top and in on the defense. But their plan failed where Larry's had succeeded, simply because Larry had provided its counter by placing a man to keep a lookout, and others where they could open a prompt rifle-fire from the cover of the pit's parapet. The attack broke under the rapid fire that met them, and the uninjured Germans scuttled back into their trench.

A fresh bombing rush was tried, and this time pushed home, in spite of the grenades that met it and filled the trench bottom with a grewsome débris of mangled men, fallen earth, and torn wire. At the end the rush was only stopped at the very parapet by Larry and his two fellows standing up and emptying their rifle magazines into the men who still crowded into the shambles trench, tearing a way through the wire and treading their own dead under foot.

More of the Stonewalls were wounded by fragments of the grenades which each man of the attackers carried and threw over into the pit before him, and one man was killed outright at the parapet by Larry's side. He was left with only four effective fighting men, and, what was worse, his stock of grenades was almost exhausted.

The end looked very near, but it was staved off a little longer by the return of one of the severely wounded men that Larry had sent back in search of help, dragging a heavy box of German stick-grenades. Nobody knew how to use these. Each grenade had a head about the size and shape of a 1-lb. jam tin attached to a wooden handle a foot long. There was no sign of any pin to pull out or any means of detonating the grenade, but Larry noticed that the end of the handle was metal-tipped and finished off with a disc with notched edges.

A quick trial showed that this unscrewed and revealed a cavity in the handle and a short, looped length of string coiled inside. Some rapid and rather risky experiments proved that a pull on the string exploded some sort of cap and started a fuse, which in turn detonated the grenade in a few seconds.

"Neat," said Harvey, the bomber. "Bloomin' neat; though I don't say as it beats the old Mills'. But, anyhow, we're dash lucky to have 'em. 'Ere they come again, Larry!"

"Sock it in," said Larry briefly. "There's more bombs than we'll have time to use, I fancy, so don't try'n save them up." He shouted orders for any of the wounded that could move themselves to clear out, and set himself to tossing over the grenades as fast as he could pull the detonating-strings.

Then his last man on the lookout on the pit rim yelled a warning and opened rapid fire, and Larry knew that another rush was coming over the open. That, he knew, was the finish, because now he had no men left to keep up a fire heavy enough to stop the rush above ground, and, if Harvey and he went to help, the ceasing of their grenade-throwing would leave the attack to come at him along the shattered trench.

He and Harvey looked once at each other, and went on grimly throwing grenades. Then Harvey dropped without a word, and Larry, looking up, saw a few Germans shooting over the pit rim. They disappeared suddenly as he looked, cut down—although he did not know that—by a heavy rifle-fire that had been opened by the British-owned trench behind him.

He yelled hoarsely at the one man left still firing from his niche up on the parapet, grabbed the box with the remaining grenades, and made a bolt across the pit for the other side and the trench opening from it. The rifleman did the same, but he fell half-way across, and Larry, reaching cover, glanced round and saw the other struggling to his knees, turned and dashed back, and half dragged, half carried the man across, up the crumbling edge of the pit, and heaved him over into the trench mouth. Then he took up his position behind the breastwork and made ready to hold it to the last possible minute.

In that last minute assistance arrived—and arrived clearly only just in time. Headed by an officer, a strong detachment of the Stonewalls, hurrying along the trench, found Larry standing waist-high above the barricade jerking the detonating-strings and hurling the last of his grenades as fast as he could throw them into the pit, from which arose a pandemonium of crashing explosions, yells and shrieks, guttural curses and the banging reports of rifles.

The Stonewalls swarmed, cheering, over the barricade and down into the hole beyond like terriers into a rat-pit. Most of the Germans there threw down their rifles and threw up their hands. The rest were killed swiftly, and the Stonewalls, with hardly a check, charged across the pit into the trench beyond, swept it clear of the enemy for a full two hundred yards, and then firmly established themselves in and across it with swiftly-built barricades and plentiful stores of bombs. Larry's share ended there, and Larry himself exited from the scene of his first command quite inconspicuously on a stretcher.

71

CHAPTER X

THE COUNTER ATTACK

Kentucky and Pug and their fellow Stonewalls fell to work energetically, their movements hastened by a galling rifle or machine-gun fire that came pelting along their trench from somewhere far out on the flank, and reaching the trench almost in enfilade, and by the warning screech and crash of some shells bursting over them. The rain had ceased a few hours before, but the trench was still sopping wet and thick with sticky mud. It was badly battered and broken down, and was little more for the most part than an irregular and shallow ditch half filled with shattered timbers, fallen earth, full and burst sandbags. Here and there were stretches of comparatively uninjured trench, deep and strongly built, but even in these, sandbags had been burst or blown out of place by shell explosions, and the walls were crumbling and shaken and tottery. The Stonewalls put in a very strenuous hour digging, refilling sandbags, piling them up, putting the trench into some sort of shape to afford cover and protection against shell and rifle fire. There was no sun, but the air was close and heavy and stagnant, and the men dripped perspiration as they worked. Their efforts began to slacken despite the urgings of the officers and non-coms., but they speeded up again as a heavier squall of shell fire shrieked up and began to burst rapidly about and above the trench.

"I was beginnin' to think this trench was good enough for anythin', and that we'd done diggin' enough," panted Pug, heaving a half-split sandbag into place, flattening it down with the blows of a broken pick-handle, and halting a moment to lift his shrapnel helmet to the

72

back of his head and wipe a dirty sleeve across his wet forehead. "But I can see that it might be made a heap safer yet."

"There's a plenty room for improvement," agreed Kentucky, wrenching and hauling at a jumble of stakes and barbed wire that had been blown in and half buried in the trench bottom. When he had freed the tangle, he was commencing to thrust and throw it out over the back of the trench when an officer passing along stopped him. "Chuck it out in front, man alive," he said. "We don't want to check our side getting in here to help us, and it's quite on the cards we may need it to help hold back the Boche presently. We're expecting a counter-attack, you know."

"Do we know?" said Pug, disgustedly, when the officer had passed along. "Mebbe you do, but I'm blowed if I know anythink about it. All I know I could put in me eye an' then not know it was there even."

"I wish I knew where Larry is, or what's happened to him," said Kentucky. "I'm some worried about him."

A string of light shells crashed overhead, another burst banging and crackling along the trench, and a procession of heavier high explosive began to drop ponderously in geyser-like spoutings of mud and earth and smoke. The Stonewalls crouched low in the trench bottom, while the ground shook under them, and the air above sang to the drone and whine of flying shell fragments and splinters. Our own guns took up the challenge, and started to pour a torrent of light and heavy shells over on to the German lines. For a time the opposing guns had matters all to themselves and their uproar completely dominated the battle. And in the brief intervals of the nearer bangs and crashes the Stonewalls could hear the deep and constant roar of gun-fire throbbing and booming and rolling in full blast up and down along the line.

"I s'pose the papers 'ud call this an ar-tillery doo-el," remarked Pug, "or re-noo-ed ar-tillery activity."

"I always thought a duel was two lots fighting each other," said a man hunkered down close in the trench bottom beside him; "but the gunners' notion of dueling seems to be to let each other alone and each hammer the other lot's infantry."

"Seems like they're passing a few packets back to each other though," said Kentucky. "Hark at that fellow up there," as a heavy

73

shell rumbled and roared over high above them, and the noise of its passing dwindled and died away, and was drowned out in the steadily sustained uproar of the nearer reports and shell bursts.

"Stand to there!" came a shout along the trench. "Look out, there, C Company.... Wait the word, then let 'em have it.... Don't waste a shot, though."

"Wot's comin' now?" said Pug, scrambling to his feet. Kentucky was already up and settling himself into position against the front wall of the parapet.

"Looks like that counter-attack we heard of," he said. "And—yes, by the Lord, some counter-attack too. Say, look at 'em, will you? Jes' look and see 'em come a-boiling."

Pug, snuggling down beside him, and pounding his elbow down on the soft earth to make a convenient elbow-rest, paused and peered out into the drifting haze of smoke that obscured the front. At first he could see nothing but the haze, starred with the quick fire flashes and thickened with the rolling clouds of our guns' shrapnel bursts. Then in the filmy gray and dun-colored cloud he saw another, a more solid and deeper colored gray bank that rolled steadily towards them.

"Gaw'strewth," he gasped. "Is that men? Is all that lump Germans? Blimey, it must be their 'ole bloomin' army comin' at us."

"There sure is a big bunch of 'em," said Kentucky. "Enough to roll us out flat if they can get in amongst us. This is where we get it in the neck if we can't stop 'em before they step into this trench. It looks ugly, Pug. Wonder why they don't give the order to fire."

"I've never bayoneted a 'Un yet," said Pug, "but mebbe I'll get a chawnce this time." He peered out into the smoke. "Can you see if they've got 'elmets on, Kentuck?" he said anxiously. "I'm fair set on one o' them 'elmets."

To Kentucky and Pug, and probably to most of the rest of the Stonewalls' rank and file, the German counter-attack boiled down into a mere matter of the rapid firing of a very hot rifle into a dense bank of smoke and a dimly seen mass of men. Each man shot straight to his front, and took no concern with what might be happening to right or left of that front. In the beginning the word

74

had been passed to set the sights at point blank and fire low, so that there was no need at any time to bother about altering ranges, and the men could devote the whole of their attention to rapid loading and firing. So each simply shot and shot and went on shooting at full speed, glancing over the sights and squeezing the trigger, jerking the bolt back and up, and pulling trigger again till the magazine was empty; then, throwing the butt down to cram a fresh clip of cartridges into the breech, swinging it up and in again to the shoulder, resuming the rapid shoot-and-load, shoot-and-load until the magazine was empty again. Each man was an automatic machine, pumping out so many bullets in so many seconds, and just because long drill and training had all gone to make the aiming and shooting mechanically correct and smooth and rapid it was mechanically deadly in its effect. And because the motions of shooting were so entirely mechanical they left the mind free to wander to other and, in many cases, ridiculously trivial things. Kentucky began to fear that his stock of cartridges would not last out, began vaguely to worry over the possibility of having to cease shooting even for a minute, until he could obtain a fresh supply. Pug was filled with an intense irritation over the behavior of his rifle, which in some mysterious fashion developed a defect in the loading of the last cartridge from each clip. The cartridge, for some reason, did not slide smoothly into the chamber, and the bolt had to be withdrawn an inch and slammed shut again each time the last cartridge came up. Probably the extra motion did not delay Pug's shooting by one second in each clip, but he was as annoyed over it as if it had reduced his rate by half. He cursed his rifle and its parts, breech, bolt, and magazine severally and distinctly, the cartridges and the clips, the men and the machinery who had made each; but at no time did he check the speed of his shooting to curse. "What's the matter?" shouted Kentucky at last. "This blasted rifle," yelled Pug angrily, jerking at the bolt and slamming it home again, "keeps stickin' all the time." Kentucky had some half-formed idea of saying that it was no good trying to shoot with a sticking rifle, and suggesting that Pug should go look for another, handing over meantime any cartridges he had left to replenish his, Kentucky's, diminishing store; but just then two men came pushing along the trench carrying a box of ammunition and throwing out a double handful of cartridges to each man. Kentucky grabbed. "Oh, good man," he said joyfully; "but say, can't you give us a few more?"

Pug glanced round at the heap flung at his elbow. "Wha's th' good o' them?" he snapped. "F'r Gawd' sake rather gimme a rifle that'll shoot."

"Rifle?" said one of the men; "there's plenty spare rifles about"; and he stooped and picked one from the trench bottom, dropped it beside Pug, and pushed on. Pug emptied his magazine, dropped his rifle, snatched up the other one, and resumed shooting. But he was swearing again before he had fired off the one clip, and that done, flung the rifle from him and grabbed his own. "Rotten thing," he growled. "It don't fit, don't set to a man's shoulder; an' it kicks like a crazy mule."

Both he and Kentucky had jerked out their sentences between shots, delaying their shooting no fraction of a second. It was only, and even then reluctantly, when there was no longer a visible target before their sights that they slowed up and stopped. And then both stayed still, with rifles pointing over the parapet, peering into the smoke ahead. Kentucky drew a long breath. "They've quit; and small blame to them."

"Got a bit more'n they bargained for, that time," said Pug exultantly, and then "Ouch!" in a sharp exclamation of pain. "What's the matter?" said Kentucky. "You feeling that arm?" "No, no," said Pug hastily, "just my elbow feelin' a bit cramped an' stiffish wi' leanin' on it."

The rifle fire was slackening and dying along the line, but the shells still whooped and rushed overhead and burst flaming and rolling out balls of white smoke over the ground in front. "Wish them guns'd knock orf a bit till we see what sorter damage we've done," said Pug. But along to the right with a rolling crash the rifles burst out into full blast again. "Look out," said Kentucky quickly, "here they come again," and he tossed muzzle over the parapet and commenced to pump bullets at the gray bulk that had become visible looming through the smoke clouds again. He was filled with eagerness to make the most of each second, to get off the utmost possible number of rounds, to score the most possible hits. He had just the same feeling, only much more intensified, that a man has at the butts when the birds are coming over fast and free. Indeed, the feeling was so nearly akin to that, the whole thing was so like shooting into driven and helpless game, the idea was so strong that the Germans were there as a target to be shot at, and he there as a shooter, that it gave him a momentary shock of utter astonishment when a bullet hit the parapet close to him and threw a spurt of mud in his face, and almost at the same instant another hit glancing on the top of his helmet, jolting it back on his head and spinning it round until the chin-strap stopped it with an unpleasant jerk on his throat. He realized suddenly, what for the moment he had completely forgotten, that he was being shot at as well as shooting, that he was as liable to be killed as one of those men out there he was pelting bullets into. Actually, of course, his risk was not one-tenth of the attackers'. He was in cover and the men advancing against the trench were doing little shooting as they came. They on the other hand were in the open, exposed full length and height, were in a solid mass through and into which the sleeting bullets drove and poured in a continuous stream. Machine-gun and rifle fire beat fiercely upon its face, while from above a deluge of high-explosive shells and tearing gusts of shrapnel fell upon it, rending and shattering and destroying. And in spite of the tempest of fire which smote it the mass still advanced. It was cut down almost as fast as it could come on, but yet not quite as fast, and the men in the trench could see the front line constantly breaking and melting away, with ragged, shifting gaps opening and closing quickly along its length, with huge mouthfuls torn out of it by the devouring shells, with whole slices and wedges cut away by the scything bullets, but still filling in the gaps, closing up the broken ranks, pressing doggedly and desperately on and in on their destroyers.

But at last the attack broke down. It had covered perhaps a hundred yards, at an appalling cost of lives, when it checked, gave slowly, and then broke and vanished. Most of the men left on their feet turned and ran heavily, but there were still some who walked, and still others who even then either refused to yield the ground they had taken or preferred the chance of shelter and safety a prone position offered rather than the heavy risk of being cut down by the bullets as they retreated. These men dropped into shell holes and craters, behind the heaps of dead, flat on the bare ground; and there some of them lay motionless, and a few, a very few, others thrust out their rifles and dared to shoot.

A heavy shell screamed over and burst just behind the Stonewalls' trench. Another and another followed in quick succession, and then, as if this had been a signal to the German guns, a tornado of shells swept roaring down upon the British line. It was the heaviest and most destructive fire the Stonewalls had yet been called upon to face. The shells were of every weight and description. The coming of each of the huge high explosives was heralded by a most appalling and nerve-shaking, long-drawn, rising torrent of noise that for the moment drowned out all the other noises of battle, and was only exceeded in its terror-inspiring volume by the rending, bellowing crash of its burst; their lesser brethren, the 5-in. and 6-in. H.E., were small by comparison, but against that their numbers were far greater, and they fell in one long pitiless succession of hammer-blows up and down the whole length of trench, filling the air with dirty black foul-smelling smoke and the sinister, vicious, and ugly sounding drone and whurr and whistle of flying splinters; and in still larger numbers the lighter shells, the shrapnel and H.E. of the field guns, the "Whizz-Bangs" and "Pip-Squeaks," swept the trench with a regular fusillade of their savage "rush-crash" explosions. The air grew dense and choking with the billowing clouds of smoke that curled and drifted about the trench, thickened and darkened until the men could hardly see a dozen yards from them.

Pug, crouched low in the bottom of the trench beside Kentucky, coughed and spluttered, "Bad's a real old Lunnon Partickler," he said, and spat vigorously.

An officer, followed by three men, crawled along the trench towards them. "Here you are, Corporal," said the officer, halting and looking over his shoulder; "this will do for you two. Get over here and out about fifty yards. Come on, the other man. We'll go over a bit further along," and he crawled off, followed by the one man.

"Wot's the game, Corp'ril?" asked Pug, as the two began to creep over the top of the parapet. "List'nin' post," said the Corporal briefly. "Goin' to lie out there a bit, in case they makes a rush through the smoke," and he and his companion vanished squirming over the shell-torn ground in front.

A few minutes later another couple of men crawled along and huddled down beside Pug. "Crump blew the trench in on some o' us along there," said one. "Buried a couple an' sent Jim an' me flyin'. Couldn't get the other two out neither. Could we, Jim?" Jim only shook his head. He had a slight cut over one eye, from which at intervals he mechanically wiped the blood with a shaking hand.

"Trench along there is a fair wreck," went on the other, then stopped and held his breath at the harsh rising roar that told of another heavy shell approaching. The four men flattened themselves to earth until the shell struck with a heavy jarring THUMP that set the ground quivering. "Dud," said two or three of them simultaneously, and "Thank God," said Kentucky, "the burst would have sure got us that time."

"Wot's that they're shoutin' along there?" said Pug anxiously. "Strewth!" and he gasped a deep breath and grabbed hurriedly for the bag slung at his side. "Gas ... 'Helmets on,' they're shoutin'."

Through the acrid odors of the explosives' fumes Kentucky caught a faint whiff of a heavy, sickly, sweet scent. Instantly he stopped breathing and, with the other three, hastily wrenched out the flannel helmet slung in its special bag by his side, pulled it over his head, and, clutching its folds tightly round his throat with one hand, tore open his jacket collar, stuffed the lower edge of the flannel inside his jacket and buttoned it up again. All four finished the oft-drilled operation at the same moment, lay perfectly quiet, inhaling the pungent odor of the impregnated flannel, and peering upward through the eye-pieces for any visible sign of the gas.

They waited there without moving for another five minutes, with the shells still pounding and crashing and hammering down all round them. Pug leaned over and put his muffled mouth close to Kentucky's ear: "They got a dead set on us here," he shouted. "Looks like our number was up this time, an's if they meant to blow this trench to blazes."

Kentucky nodded his cowled head. It did look as if the German gunners were determined to completely obliterate that portion of the trench, but meantime—it was very ridiculous, of course, but there it was—his mind was completely filled with vague gropings in his memory to recall what perfume it was that the scent of the gas reminded him of. He puzzled over it, recalling scent after scent in vain, sure that he was perfectly familiar with it, and yet unable to place it. It was most intensely and stupidly irritating.

The shell fire worked up to a pitch of the most ferocious intensity. None actually hit the portion of trench the four were in, but several came dangerously close in front, behind, and to either side of them. The wall began to crumble and shake down in wet clods and crumblings, and at the burst of one shell close out in front, a large piece broke off the front edge and fell in, followed by a miniature landslide of falling earth. The trench appeared to be on the point of collapsing and falling in on them.

"We gotter move out o' this!" shouted Pug, "else we'll be buried alive."

"What's the good of ... don't believe there's any one left but us ...

79

better get out of it," said the man Jim. His voice was muffled and indistinct inside his helmet, but although the others only caught fragments of his sentences his meaning was plain enough. The four looked at each other, quite uselessly, for the cowl-like helmets masked all expression and the eyes behind the celluloid panes told nothing. But instinctively they looked from one to the other, poking and twisting their heads to bring one another within the vision range of the eye-pieces, so that they looked like some strange ghoulish prehistoric monsters half-blind and wholly horrible. Jim's companion mumbled something the others could not hear, and nodded his shapeless head slightly. His vote was for retirement, for although it had not been spoken, retirement was the word in question in the minds of all. Kentucky said nothing. True, it appeared that to stay there meant destruction; it appeared, too, that the Stonewalls as a fighting force must already be destroyed ... and ... and ... violets! was it the scent of violets? No, not violets; but some flower....

Pug broke in. "There's no orders to retire," he said. "There's no orders to retire," and poked and turned his head, peering at one after the other of them. "We carn't retire when there ain't no orders," waggling his pantomimic head triumphantly as if he had completely settled the matter. But their portion of trench continued to cave in alarmingly. A monster shell falling close out on their right front completed the destruction. The trench wall shivered, slid, caught and held, slid again, and its face crumbled and fell in. The four saw it giving and scrambled clear. They were almost on the upper ground level now, but the hurried glances they threw round showed nothing but the churned up ground, the drifting curling smoke-wreaths, tinted black and green and yellow and dirty white, torn whirling asunder every few moments by the fresh shell bursts which in turn poured out more billowing clouds. No man of the Stonewalls, no man at all, could be seen, and the four were smitten with a sudden sense of loneliness, of being left abandoned in this end-of-the-world inferno. Then the man Jim noticed something and pointed. Dimly through the smoke to their left they saw one man running half doubled up, another so stooped that he almost crawled. Both wore kilts, and both moved forward. In an instant they disappeared, but the sight of them brought new life and vigor to the four.

"The Jocks that was on our left," shouted Pug, "gettin' outer the trench into shell-holes. Good enough, too. Come on."

They did not have far to seek for a shell-hole. The ground was covered with them, the circle of one in many cases cutting the circle of the next. There were many nearer available, but Pug sheered to his left and ran for the place he had seen the two Highlanders disappear, and the others followed. There were plenty of bullets flying, but in the noise of shell-fire the sound of their passing was drowned, except the sharp, angry hiss of the nearer ones and the loud smacks of those that struck the ground about them.

They had less than a dozen yards to cover, but in that short space two of them went down. Jim's companion was struck by a shell splinter and killed instantly. Pug, conscious only of a violent blow on the side, fell, rolling from the force of the stroke. But he was up and running on before Kentucky had well noticed him fall, and when they reached the shell-hole and tumbled into it almost on top of the two Highlanders there, Pug, cautiously feeling round his side, discovered his haversack slashed and torn, its contents broken and smashed flat. "Fust time I've been glad o' a tin o' bully," he shouted, exhibiting a flattened tin of preserved meat. "But I s'pose it was the biscuits that was really the shell-proof bit."

"Are you hurt at all?" said Kentucky. "Not a ha'porth," said Pug. "Your pal was outed though, wasn't 'e, chum?"

The other man nodded. "... cross the neck ... 'is 'ead too ... as a stone...."

"You're no needin' them," said one of the Highlanders suddenly. "It's only tear-shells—no the real gas."

The others noticed then that they were wearing the huge goggles that protect the eyes from "tear," or lachrymatory shells, and the three Stonewalls exchanged their own helmets for the glasses with huge relief.

"What lot are you?" said one of the Scots. "Oh, ay; you're along on oor right, aren't ye?"

"We was," said Pug; "but I 'aven't seen one o' ours since this last shell strafin' began. I'm wondering if there's any left but us three. Looks like our trench was blotted out."

But on that he was corrected swiftly and dramatically. The pouring shells ceased suddenly to crash over and about them, continued only to rush, shrieking and yelling, high above their heads. At the same moment a figure appeared suddenly from the ground a little in front of them, and came running back. He was passing their shelter when Kentucky recognized him as the officer who earlier had moved along the trench to go out in front and establish a listening post. He caught sight of the little group at the same moment, swerved, and ran in to them. "Look out," he said; "another attack coming. You Stonewalls? Where's our trench? Further back, isn't it?"

"What's left of it, sir," said Kentucky. "Mighty near blotted out, though."

"Open fire," said the officer. "Straight to your front. You'll see 'em in a minute. I must try'n find the others."

But evidently the word of warning had reached the others, for a sharp crackle of rifle fire broke out along to the right, came rattling down towards them in uneven and spasmodic bursts. The men in the shell-hole lined its edge and opened fire, while the officer trotted on. A dozen paces away he crumpled and fell suddenly, and lay still. In the shell-hole they were too busy to notice his fall, but from somewhere further back, out of the smoke-oozing, broken ground, a couple of figures emerged at the double, halted by the limp figure, lifted and carried it back.

"There's still some of us left," said Pug, cheerfully, as they heard the jerky rifle fire steady down and commence to beat out in the long roll of independent rapid fire.

"Not too many, though," said Kentucky anxiously. "And it took us all our time to stand 'em off before," he added significantly. He turned to the two Highlanders, who were firing coolly and methodically into the thinning smoke. "Can you see 'em yet?"

"No," said one, without turning his head; "but we've plenty cairtridges ... an' a bullet gangs straight enough withoot seein'." And he and the other continued to fire steadily.

Then suddenly a puff of wind thinned and lifted the smoke cloud, and at the same instant all saw again that grim gray wall rolling down upon them. The five rifles in the pit crashed together, the bolts clicked back, and the brass cartridge-cases winked out and fell; and before they had ceased to roll where they dropped the five rifles were banging again, and the five men were plying bolt and trigger for dear life. Behind them and to the right and left other rifles were drumming and roaring out a furious fire, and through their noise rose the sharp tat-tat-tat-tat of the machine guns. The British artillery, too, had evidently seen their target, the observers had passed back the corrections of range and rapid sequence of orders, and the bellowing guns began to rake and batter the advancing mass.

But this time they had an undue share of the work to do. For all the volume and rapidity of the infantry fire, it was quickly plain that its weight was not nearly as great as before, that the intense preparatory bombardment had taken heavy toll of the defenders, that this time the attack had nothing like the numbers to overcome that it had met and been broken by before. Again the advancing line shredded and thinned as before under the rifle and shell fire, but this time the gaps were quicker filled; the whole line came on at greater speed. In the pit the five men shot with desperate haste, but Kentucky at least felt that their effort was too weak, that presently the advancing tide must reach and overwhelm them. Although other shell-holes to right and left were occupied as theirs was they were slightly in advance of the ragged line, and must be the first to be caught. There was nothing left them apparently but to die fighting. But if the others saw this they gave no sign of it—continued merely to fire their fastest.

One of the Highlanders exclaimed suddenly, half rose, and dropped again to his knees. The blood was welling from a wound in his throat, but as his body sagged sideways he caught himself with a visible effort, and his hands, which had never loosed their grip on the rifle, fumbled at the breech a moment, and slipped in a fresh clip of cartridges. He gulped heavily, spat out a great mouthful of frothy blood, spoke thickly and in gasps, "Hey, Mac ... tak' her, for ... the last. The magazine's full ..." And he thrust out the rifle to the other Scot with a last effort, lurched sideways, and slid gently down in the bottom of the pit. The other man caught the rifle quickly, placed it by his side, and resumed firing. The others never ceased for a moment to load and fire at top speed. Plainly there was no time to attend to the dead or wounded when they themselves were visibly near the end the other had met.

The German line was coming in under the guard of the shells that the gunners dared not drop closer for fear of hitting their own line. The rifles were too few to hold back the weight of men that were coming in now in a scattered rush.

83

Pug cursed wrathfully. "I do b'lieve the blighters is goin' to get in on us," he said; and by his tone one might suppose he had only just realized the possibility; was divided between astonishment and anger at it. Kentucky, who had looked on the possibility as a certainty for some little time back, continued to pick a man of the advancing line, snap-shoot hurriedly at him, load and pick another target. And away somewhere in the back of his mind his thoughts worked and worried at the old, irritating puzzle—"Lilies, no; but something like them ... heavy, sweetish ... not lilies ... what other flower, now ..."; Jim, the third Stonewall, glanced back over his shoulder. "Why can't them fellows back there shoot a bit quicker?" he said irritably. "They'll have this lot a-top o' us if they don't look out." Kentucky, his fingers slipping in a fresh cartridge-clip, his eye singling out a fresh mark, was slightly amused to notice that this man, too, seemed surprised by the possibility of the Germans breaking through their fire; and all the while "... lilac, stocks, honeysuckle, hyacinth ... hyacinth, hyacinth, no ..."; the Scot lifted the dead man's rifle and put it on the ledge at his right elbow.

"Strewth," said Pug, with confident cheerfulness. "Won't our chaps make them 'Uns squeal when they gets close enough for the baynit?"

The shells continued to rush and scream overhead, and burst in and over the mass of the attackers. But the front line was well in under this defense now, scrambling and struggling over the broken ground. The nearest groups were within thirty to forty yards.

They were near enough now for the bombers to come into play, and from the scattered shell-holes along the British line little black objects began to whirl and soar out into the air, and the sharp crashes of the exploding Mills' grenades rose rapidly into a constant shattering series that over-ran and drowned out the rolling rifle fire. The ground out in front belched quick spurts of flame and smoke, boiled up anew in another devil's cauldron of destruction.

The advancing Germans were for the moment hidden again behind the swirling smoke bank, but now they too were using their bombs, and the stick-grenades came sailing out of the smoke; curving over, bombing down and rolling or bucketing end over end to burst about the British line. One fell fairly in the shell-crater beside Kentucky, and he had only bare time to grab at it, snatch it up and fling it clear before it burst. And yet, even as he snatched half expecting the thing to go off in his hand, his mind was still running on the memory quest after the elusive name of that scent he had forgotten.

84

The German line emerged from the smoke, raggedly but yet solidly enough to overwhelm the weakened defense. Plainly this was the end.

"Roses," said Kentucky, suddenly and triumphantly. "Roses—tuberoses. That's it exactly."

CHAPTER XI

FORWARD OBSERVING

Among the stock situations of the melodrama, one of the most worked to death is that of the beleaguered garrison at the last gasp, and the thrilling arrival of the rescuing force at the critical moment. It is so old and threadbare now that probably no theater would dare stage it; but in the war the same situation has been played again and again in the swaying and straining lines of battle in every variety of large and small scale. What the theater has rejected as too theatrical, the artificial as too artificial, the real has accepted as so much a commonplace that it is hardly remarked. Actually the battle line is one long series of critical situations on one side or the other, the timely arrival, or failure to arrive, of assistance at the critical moment. The great difference is that in the theater the rescue never fails to arrive, in war it often does.

Certainly the Stonewalls were as near the last gasp as ever dramatist would dare bring his crisis; but when their rescue came they were too busy helping it, too busy pushing the Germans back into what they hoped would be a similar unpleasant situation (without the timely rescue) to bother about it being a "dramatic situation" at all.

The Scot and the three Stonewalls shooting from the shell crater a little in front of the thin and scattered line were close enough to the front groups of the advancing German line to distinguish the features of the men's faces, when they were suddenly aware that the groups were going down: were vanishing from before their eyes, that the charging line came no nearer, that its front, if anything, receded. The front lines were being cut down now faster than they could advance, and the lines which fell dropped out of the low vision line of the defenders, and were hidden in the low-hanging smoke haze and in the welter of shell-pits, furrows, and heaps of earth over which the advance moved. The sound of the rifle fire swelled suddenly and heavily; the air grew vibrant with the hiss and zipp of bullets.

The four in the shell pit continued to give all their attention to rapid shooting until the sound of running footsteps and shouting voices made them turn. All along the line to right and left of them they could see figures running forward in short rushes, halting to fire, running on again, dropping into holes and opening a rapid fire from their cover. Into the pit beside the four tumbled three men one after another, panting and blowing, but shouting and laughing. "Cheer oh, mates," called one. "Give us a bit o' room on the front edge there, will you?" Each of the three carried some burden. They clustered closely together a moment, but with a delay of no more than seconds stood up and began to hoist into position on the pit's edge a light machine gun. "Let 'er rip, Bill," said one, who wore the tunic of an officer; and Bill, crouching behind his gun, started to "let 'er rip" in a stream of fire jets and clattering reports.

"You boys were pretty near the limit, eh?" said the officer. "Mighty near," said Kentucky; "you just sat into the game in time to stop 'em scooping the pool, sir."

"Hey, Chick, get a move on wi' that loadin' there," said Bill; "you're hardly keepin' the ol' coffee mill grindin'."

"You're Anzacs, ain't you?" said Pug, noticing the shirt-tunic the officer wore. Bill was bare-headed; Chick wore a metal helmet crammed down on top of his slouch hat.

"That's what," said Chick, feverishly busy with his loading. "What crowd are you?"

"Fifth Sixth Stonewalls," said Pug.

"You was damn near bein' First 'n' Last Stone-colds this trip," said Chick. "Good job we buzzed in on you."

A few yards away another machine gun, peering over the edge of a shell crater, broke out in frantic chattering reports.

"That's Bennet's gun, I expect," said the officer; "I'll just slide over and see how he goes. Keep her boiling here, and mind you don't move out of this till you get the word."

Chick nodded. "Right-oh!" he said, and the officer climbed out of the hole and ran off.

For another minute or two the machine gun continued to spit its stream of bullets. "They're breaking again," said Kentucky suddenly; "my Lord, look how the guns are smashing them."

The attack broke and fell back rapidly, with the running figures stumbling and falling in clusters under the streaming bullets and hailing shrapnel. In less than half a minute the last running man had disappeared, the ground was bare of moving figures, but piled with dead and with those too badly wounded to crawl into cover.

"First round to us," said Bill cheerfully, and cut off the fire of his gun. "An' last move to a good many o' them blokes out there," said Chick; "they fairly got it in the neck that time. I haven't seen such a bonzer target to strafe since we was in G'llipoli."

"Is there many o' you chaps here?" said Pug. "Dunno rightly," said Chick, producing a packet of cigarettes. "'Bout time for a smoke-oh, ain't it, Bill?"

"I'm too blame dry to smoke," said Bill. "Wonder wot we're waitin' 'ere for now. D'you think the other battalions is up?"

"Have you heard anything about how the show is going?" said Kentucky.

"Good-oh, they tell us," said Chick. "We saw a big bunch o' prisoners back there a piece, an' we hear there's two or three villages taken. We came up here to take some other village just in front here. I s'pose they'll loose us on it presently."

There was a short lull in the gunfire, and the noisy passage of the shells overhead slowed down. A shout was heard: "Close in on your right, Stonewalls. Rally along to the right."

"Hear that?" said Pug, "there is some Stonewalls left, then. Blimey, if I wasn't beginnin' to think we was the sole survivors."

"We'd best move along," said Kentucky, and the three made ready.

"Well, so long, mates," said Chick, and "See you in Berlin—or the nex' world," said Bill lightly.

"To your right, Stonewalls; close to your right," came the shout again, and the three clambered out of their hole and doubled in across the torn ground to their right. There were other men doing the same, stooped low, and taking advantage of any cover they found, and gradually the remains of the battalion gathered loosely together, in and about the remains of the old trench. Pug and Kentucky anxiously questioned every man they met as to whether they had seen anything of Larry Arundel, but could get no tidings of him. The battalion was rapidly if roughly sorted out into its groups of companies, and when this was done and there were no signs of Larry, little could be concluded but that he had been killed or wounded. "He'd sure have been looking for us," said Kentucky; "I'm afraid he's a wash-out." "Looks like it," said Pug sadly. "But mebbe he's only wounded. Let's hope it's a cushy one."

The guns were opening behind them again, and bombarding with the utmost violence a stretch of the ground some little distance in front. "It's a village we're to take," one of the sergeants told them. "That was our objective when the German counter-attack stopped us. We were to attack, with the Anzacs in support. Suppose we're going on with the original program; but we're pretty weak to tackle the job now. Hope the Jocks on the left didn't get it too bad."

"Should think we was due for a bit of an ease-off," said Pug. "It's long past my usual desh-oo-nay time as it is."

An officer moved along the line. "Now, boys, get ready," he said, "the next bit's the last. Our turn's over when we take this village. Make a quick job of it."

In front of them the ground was shrouded again with drifting smoke, and out beyond the broken ground and the remains of a shattered parapet they could see the flashing fires and belching smoke clouds of the shells that continued to pour over and down. In a minute or two the fire lifted back from the belt where it had been thundering, and at that the Stonewalls, with the Highlanders to one side and another regiment to the other, rose and began to advance. From their front there came little opposition, but from somewhere out on the flank a rain of machine-gun bullets swept driving down upon them. The Stonewalls pushed on doggedly. It was heavy going,

89

for the ground was torn and plowed up in innumerable furrows and pits and holes and ridges, laced with clutching fragments of barbed-wire, greasy and slippery with thick mud. The Stonewalls went on slowly but surely, but on their right the other regiment, which had perhaps caught the heavier blast of fire, checked a little, struggled on again gamely, with men falling at every step, halted, and hastily sought cover amongst the shell holes. The Stonewalls persisted a little longer and went a little further, but the fire grew fiercer and faster, and presently they too, with the Highlanders on their left, flung down pantingly into such cover as they could find.

Kentucky and Pug had struggled along together, and sought shelter from the storming bullets in the same deep shell hole. Three minutes later an officer crawled over the edge and tumbled in after them. He was wounded, the blood streaming from a broken hand, a torn thigh, and a bullet wound in the neck.

"One of you will have to go back," he said faintly; "I can't go further. You, Lee," and he nodded at Kentucky; "d'you think you can take a message through to the gunners?"

"Why, sure," said Kentucky, promptly. "Leastways, I can try."

So the officer crawled to the edge of the pit and pointed to where, amongst some scattered mounds of earth, they had located the nest of machine guns. Then he pointed the direction Kentucky must take to find the Forward Observing Officer of Artillery. "About a hundred yards behind that last trench we were in," said the officer. "Look, you can see a broken bit of gray wall. Get back to there if you can, and tell the officer where these machine guns are. Tell him they're holding us up and the C.O. wants him to turn every gun he can on there and smash them up. Take all the cover you can. You can see it's urgent we get the message through, and I don't know where any of the regular runners are."

"Right, sir," said Kentucky; "I'll get it through." He nodded to Pug, "S'long, Pug," and Pug nodded back, "So long, Kentuck. Goo' luck." Kentucky scrambled from the hole and went off, crouching and dodging and running. No other man was showing above ground, and as he ran he felt most horribly lonely and appallingly exposed. He took what cover he could, but had to show himself above ground most of the time, because he gained little in safety and lost much in time by jumping in and out of the shell holes. So he skirted the

90

larger ones and ran on, and came presently to the line of Anzacs waiting to support. He hardly waited to answer the eager questions they threw him, but hurried on, crossed the ruined fragments of the old trench, found presently a twisted shallow gully that appeared to run in the direction he wanted, ducked into it, and pushed on till he came almost abreast of the gray wall. He had to cross the open again to come to it, and now, with a hazy idea that it would be a pity to fail now, took infinite precautions to crawl and squirm from hole to hole, and keep every scrap of cover he could. He reached the wall at last and crept round it, exulting in his success. He looked round for the officer—and saw no one. A shock of amazement, of dismay, struck him like a blow. He had struggled on with the one fixed idea so firmly in his mind, looking on the gray wall so definitely as his goal, measuring the distance to it, counting the chances of reaching it, thinking no further than it and the delivery of his message there, that for a moment he felt as lost, as helpless as if the sun had vanished at noon. He was just recovering enough to be beginning to curse his luck and wonder where he was to look for the lost officer when a loud voice made him jump. "Section fire ten seconds," it said, and a moment later a hollow and muffled voice repeated tonelessly: "Section fire ten seconds." Kentucky looked round him. A dead man sprawled over the edge of a shell hole, a boot and leg protruded from behind some broken rubble, but no living man was in sight, although the voices had sounded almost elbow close.

"Hullo," said Kentucky loudly. "Artillery. Where are you, sir?"

"Hullo," answered the voice. "Who is there?" and from a tumbled pile of sandbags at the end of the broken wall a head was cautiously raised. "Do you want me? Keep down out of sight. I don't want this place spotted."

Kentucky was creeping carefully towards him when a sepulchral voice from underground somewhere made him jump. "Beg pardon, sir. Didn't catch that last order, sir."

"All right, Ridley," said the officer. "I was talking to some one up here"; and to Kentucky, "What is it?"

Kentucky gave his message briefly. "Right," said the officer, pulling out a soiled map. "Come along beside me here, and see if you can point the spot from here. Careful now. Keep down. If they spot this for an Oh Pip[2] they'll shell us off the earth."

---

[2] O.P. Observation Post.

The officer was a young man, although under the mask of dirt and mud splashes and unshaven chin he might have been any age. He was sprawled against a broken-down breastwork of fallen bricks and timber, with a rough strengthening and buttressing of sandbags, and an irregular shaped opening opposite his head to look out from. Kentucky sidled to the opening and looked long and carefully for landmarks on the smoke-clouded ground before him. He found the task difficult, because here he was on slightly higher ground, from which the aspect appeared utterly different to the little he had seen of it from below. But at last he was able to trace more or less the points over which he had passed, to see some of the Anzacs crouching in their cover and moving cautiously about behind it, and from that to locate the Stonewalls' position and the rough earth heaps—which now he could see formed part of an irregular line of trench—where the machine-guns were supposed to be. He pointed the place out to the officer, who looked carefully through his glasses, consulted his map, looked out again.

"Likely enough spot," he commented. "It's been well strafed with shell fire already, but I suppose they have their guns down in deep dugouts there. Anyhow, we'll give 'em another going over. Ridley!"

"Sir," answered the voice from below. "Stop. Fresh target. Machine-guns in trench. All guns...." and followed a string of orders about degrees and yards which Kentucky could not follow. "Now you watch the spot," said the officer when the voice had reported "All ready, sir," and he had settled himself in position with glasses to his eyes. "Watch and see if the shells land about the place you think the guns are." He passed an order to fire, and a few seconds later said sharply, "There! See them?"

But Kentucky had not seen them, and had to confess it. Or rather he had not seen these particular bursts to be sure of them, because the whole air was puffing and spurting with black smoke and white smoke and yellowish smoke.

"They were a bit left and beyond where I wanted 'em," said the officer. "We'll try again. I'm firing four guns together. Look for four white smoke bursts in a bunch somewhere above your earth heaps."

"See them?" "I got 'em," exclaimed the officer and Kentucky simultaneously a moment later. Kentucky was keyed up to an excited elation. This was a new game to him, and he was enjoying it thoroughly. He thought the four bursts were exactly over the spot required, but the more experienced observer was not so satisfied, and went on feeling for his target with another couple of rounds before he was content. But then he called for high explosive, and proceeded to deluge the distant trench with leaping smoke clouds, flashes of fire, and whirlwinds of dust and earth. Kentucky watched the performance with huge satisfaction, and began to regret that he had not joined the artillery. It was so much better, he concluded, to be snugly planted in a bit of cover calling orders to be passed back per telephone and watching the shells play on their target. He was soon to find that this was not quite all the gunners' business. He ducked suddenly back from the lookout as a shower of bullets threshed across the ground, swept up to the broken wall, and hailed rattling and lashing on and round it. The hail continued for some seconds and stopped suddenly. "Some beast out there," said the officer reflectively, "has his suspicions of this spot. That's the third dose I've had in the last half-hour. Machine gun."

He went on with his firing, watching through his glass and shouting corrections of aim to the signaler below if a gun went off its target. Another shower of bullets clattered against the stones, and two spun ricocheting and shrieking through the loophole. Kentucky began to think observing was hardly the safe and pleasant job he had imagined. "Afraid my little eighteen-pounder pills won't make enough impression there, if they're in dug-outs," said the officer. "Think I'll go 'n ask the Brigade to turn the Heavies on to that lot. If you're going back you can tell your C.O. I'm fixing it all right, and we'll give 'em a good hammering."

A shell shrieked up and burst close overhead, followed in quick succession by another and another.

"Better wait a bit before you start," said the Forward Officer. "Looks as if they might be making it hot round here for a bit. Come along below while I talk to the Brigade. Carefully now. Don't let 'em spot you."

The two crawled back, and then dived down a steep stair into a deep dug-out. Close to the entrance a telephonist sat on the ground with an instrument beside him. The officer squatted beside him and worked the "buzzer" for a minute, and then explained the situation to whoever was at the other end.

"That's all right," he said at the finish. "The Heavies are going to hot 'em a bit. You'd better wait a little longer," he continued, as the dug-out quivered to a muffled crash somewhere above them. "They're still pasting us. I'm going up to observe for the Heavies," he said, turning to the signaler. "You just pass my orders back and the battery will put them through."

He disappeared up the narrow stair just as another heavy shell crashed down. The signaler set his instrument beside him, lifted the receiver to his head, and leaned back wearily against the wall. "Are you ready, sir?" he shouted a moment later, and faintly the officer's reply came back to them, "All ready," and was repeated into the telephone. A moment later, "Fired, sir," the signaler shouted, and after a pause down came the officer's remarks, to be repeated back word for word.

Once Kentucky started up the stairs, but on reaching the open he heard what had failed to penetrate to the dug-out, the loud whistling screams of shells, the sharp crack of their overhead burst, the clash and thump of the flying fragments on the stones and ground. Kentucky came down the steps again. "Bit warm up there, ain't it?" said the signaler, continuing to hold the receiver to his ear, but placing his hand over the mouthpiece in speaking to Kentucky.

"Mighty warm," said Kentucky. "I don't fancy your officer's job up top there in the open."

The signaler yawned widely. "He's the second to-day," he said. "One expended to date—bit o' shrap—killed straight out."

"You look kind of tuckered out," said Kentucky, looking at the man. "I'm nex' door to doin' the sleep-walkin' act," said the signaler. He passed another order. "We bin shootin' like mad for a week. Not too much sleep, going all the time, an' I 'aven't shut my eyes since yesterday morning."

Another shell hit the ground close outside, and some fragments of stone and dirt pattered down the stair.

"Can't say I like this," said Kentucky restlessly. "If a shell plunked into that entrance or bust it in where'd we be?"

"That's easy," said the telephonist. "We'd be here, an' likely to stay here," and raised his voice again to shout a message to the officer.

They sat another five minutes with the walls shivering slightly or quaking violently as the shells fell close or at a distance. The telephonist sat apparently half-asleep, his eyes vacant, and his shoulders rounded, his voice raised at times to shout to the Forward Officer, sunk again to a monotonous drawl repeating the officer's words into the telephone. Once he glanced at Kentucky and spoke briefly. "Why don't you get down to it an' 'ave a kip?" he said. And when Kentucky said he didn't feel particularly sleepy, and anyhow must move along in five or ten minutes, "My Gawd," said the telephonist; "not sleepy! An' missin' a chance for ten minutes' kip. My Gawd!"

When the shelling appeared to have slackened Kentucky crawled up the stair, and after a word with the officer set out on his return journey. Ahead where he judged the German position to be he could see a swirling cloud of dirty smoke, torn asunder every moment by quick-following flashes and springing fountains of earth and more belching smoke-clouds that towered upward in thick spreading columns, and thinned and rolled outward again to add still further to the dirty reek. The earth shook to the clamorous uproar of the guns, the air pulsed to the passage of countless shells, their many-toned but always harsh and strident shriekings. The greater weight of metal was from the British side, but as he hurried forward, stumbling and slipping over the wet and broken ground, Kentucky heard every now and then the rush and crash of German shells bursting near him. The rolling, pealing thunder of the guns, the thuds and thumps and bangings of their and their shells' reports, were so loud and so sustained that they drowned the individual sounds of approaching shells, and several times Kentucky was only aware of their burst on seeing the black spout of earth and smoke, on hearing the flying fragments sing and whine close past or thud into the wet ground near him.

He toiled on and came at last to an enormous shell crater in which a full dozen of the Anzacs squatted or stood. He halted a moment to speak to them, to ask how things were going. He found he had come through the main Anzac line without knowing it, so broken and uptorn was the ground, and so well were the men concealed in the deeper scattered holes. This dozen men were well in advance and close up on the line which held the Stonewalls and which they were supporting.

"Your mob is just about due to slam at 'em again, mate," said a sergeant, looking at his wrist-watch. "You'd better hustle some if you want to go to it along wi' yer own cobbers. There goes the guns liftin' now. Time, gentlemen, please," and he snapped down the cover of his watch and stood to look out.

Kentucky climbed out and ran on. The thunder of the guns had not ceased for an instant, but the fire-flashes and spurting smoke clouds no longer played about the same spot as before. The guns had lifted their fire and were pouring their torrent of shells further back behind the spot marked for assault. Now, as Kentucky knew well, was the designed moment for the attack, and he looked every moment to see a line of figures rise and move forward. But he saw nothing except the tumbled sea of broken ground, saw no sign of rising men, no sign of movement. For full two or three minutes he hunted for the Stonewalls, for the line he wanted to rejoin; and for those precious minutes no beat of rifle fire arose, no hail of bullets swept the ground over which the attack should pass. Then a machine gun somewhere in the haze ahead began to chatter noisily, and, quickly, one after another joined it and burst into a streaming fire that rose rapidly to a steady and unbroken roar. Shells began to sweep and crash over the open too, and Kentucky ducked down into a deep shell-hole for cover.

"What's gone wrong?" he wondered. "They were sure meant to start in when the guns lifted, and they'd have been well across by this. Now the Boche machine-gunners have had time to haul the guns from their dug-outs and get busy. What's wrong? Surely the battalion hasn't been clean wiped out."

He peered cautiously over the edge of his hole, but still he saw no sign of movement. He was completely puzzled. Something was wrong, but what? The Anzacs had told him the attack was due, and those lifting guns had backed their word. And yet there was no attack. He waited for long minutes—minutes empty of attack, empty of sign, empty of everything except the raving machine guns and the storming bullets.

CHAPTER XII

A VILLAGE AND A HELMET

Kentucky decided that it was as useless as it was unnecessary for him to remain alone in his exposed position, and forthwith proceeded to crawl back to where he knew that at least he would find some one. So, keeping as low as possible, he started back, dodging from shell hole to shell hole. In about the fourth one he came to he found a group of several men, all dead, and plainly killed by the one low-bursting shell. He could see that they were Stonewalls, too, and began to wonder if the reason for his failing to find the line was the simple one that the line no longer existed. It was a foolish supposition perhaps, but men are prone to such after long day and night strain in a hot action, are even more prone to it under such circumstances as brought Kentucky to this point of crouching on the edge of a shell-hole with sudden death whistling and crashing and thundering in his ears, spread horribly under his eyes. He shivered, skirted round the pit, and over into the next one, just as another man stepped crouching over its edge. Kentucky saw him, and with a sense of enormous relief recognized him too as one of the Stonewalls' officers. Here at last was some one he knew, some one who knew him, some one who would tell him perhaps what had happened, would certainly tell him what to do, give him simple orders to be simply obeyed. The officer was a boy with a full quarter less years to his age than Kentucky himself had, a lad who in normal life would probably still have been taking orders from a schoolmaster, who certainly, instead of giving, would have been taking orders or advice from a man his equal in education, more

97

than his equal in age and worldliness, as Kentucky was. And yet Kentucky saw him with something of the relief a lost child would feel to meet his mother, and the officer was as natural in giving his orders as if Kentucky were the child. There is nothing unusual in all this. I only mention it because its very usualness is probably odd to any one outside the Service, and is likely to be little realized by them.

"I'm mighty glad to see you, sir," said Kentucky. "I thought I'd clean lost the battalion."

"The battalion's strung out along here," said the officer. "But I'm just passing along orders to retire a little on the supporting line behind us. So just push along back, and pass the word to do the same to any of ours you run across." He moved on without further word, and Kentucky continued his rearward journey. He was aiming for the same lot of men he had passed through on his way forward, but in the broken litter of ground missed them, and instead ran on another group of half a dozen sheltering in another deep shell crater. He explained to them that in obedience to orders he had retired to join their line.

"Well, you got to keep on retirin', mate," said one of them sulkily, "if you're going to hitch in with us. We just got the office too that we're to take the back track."

"Hope it's all right," said another doubtfully. "Seems so dash crazy to push up here and then go back for nix."

"That Curly's such a loose-tiled kid, he might easy have mistook the order," said another.

"Anyway," said the first, "this bloke says 'im an' 'is cobbers is hittin' out for the back paddock, and——"

"What's that?" several interrupted simultaneously, and moved eagerly to the crater edge. Clear through the rolling rifle and gun-fire came a shrill "Coo-ee," and then another and another, louder and nearer. Kentucky scrambled to the edge with the others and looked out. Down to their right they could see figures climbing out of shell holes, starting up from the furrows, moving at the run forward, and again they heard the shrill "coo-ee's" and a confusion of shouts and calls. Kentucky saw the half-dozen Anzacs scrambling from their hole like scared cats going over a fence, scuffling and jostling in their haste, heard them shouting and laughing like children going to a school treat. "Come on, mates ... nix on the back track ... play up, Anzacs...." For a moment Kentucky was puzzled. He had plain orders to retire to the support line. "Come on, cully," shouted the last man out, looking back at him—but if the support line was advancing—"... your bunch is mixin' it with us." He paused to catch up and fling along the line the coo-ee that came ringing down again, hitched his rifle forward, and doubled off after the others. Kentucky climbed out and followed him. At first the whistle and shriek and snap-snap of bullets was continuous, and it seemed impossible that he should continue without being hit, that each step he took must be the last. He wondered where the bullet would hit him, whether it would hurt much, whether he would have to wait long for the stretcher-bearers. He slackened his pace at sight of an Anzac officer rolling on the ground, coughing and spitting up frothy blood. But the Anzac saw his pause, and gathered strength to wave him on, to clear his choking throat and shout thickly to "Go on, boy; go on. I'm all right. Give 'em hell." Kentucky ran on. The bullets were fewer now, although the roar of firing from in front seemed to grow rather than slacken. His breath came heavily. The ground was rough and killingly slippery. He was nearly done up; but it was crazy to slow down there in the open; must keep on. He caught up one of the groups in front and ran with them. They were shouting ... where did they get the wind to shout ... and how much further was it to the trench? Then he saw the men he ran with begin to lift their rifles and fire or shoot from the hip as they ran; he saw gray coats crawling from a dug-out a dozen yards to his left, and with a shock realized that there was no trench to cross, that the shells must have leveled it, that he was actually into the enemy position. He ran on, heavily and at a jog-trot, without a thought of where he was running to or why he ran. He didn't think; merely ran because the others did. He stopped, too, when they stopped, and began to fire with them at a little crowd of Germans who emerged suddenly from nowhere and came charging down at them. Several Germans fell; the others kept on, and Kentucky saw one of them swing a stick bomb to throw. Kentucky shot him before he threw—shot with his nerves suddenly grown steel strong, his brain cool, his eye clear, his hand as steady as rock. He shot again and dropped the man who stooped to pick the bomb that fell from the other's hand. Then the bomb exploded amongst them. There were only four standing when the smoke cleared, and the Anzacs were running at them with bayonets at the level. There were only three Anzacs now, but the Germans threw their hands up. Then when the Anzacs slowed to a walk and came to within arm's length, with their bayonet points up, one of the Germans dropped his hand and flashed out a pistol. Kentucky shot him before he could fire. He had not run in with the others, and was a score of paces away, and one of the Anzacs half-hid the man with the pistol. But he shot knowing—not believing, or thinking, or hoping, but knowing he would kill. It was his day, he was "on his shoot," he couldn't miss. The other Germans dropped their hands too, but whether to run or fight—the bayonet finished them without a chance to answer that. "Come on, Deadeye," shouted one of the Anzacs; and when Kentucky joined them, "Some shootin', that. I owe you one for it too."

They went on again, but there was little more fighting. Anyhow, Kentucky didn't fight. He just shot; and whatever he shot at he hit, as surely and certainly as Death itself. There were a great many dead Germans lying about, and the ground was one churned heap of broken earth and shell-holes. They came suddenly on many men in khaki, walking about and shouting to each other. Then a Stonewall corporal met him and pointed to where the Stonewalls were gathering, and told him he had better go join them, and Kentucky trudged off towards them feeling all of a sudden most desperately tired and done up, and most horribly thirsty. The first thing he asked when he reached the Stonewalls was whether any one had a drop of water to spare; and then he heard a shout, a very glad and cheery shout that brought a queer, warm glow to his heart, "Kentuck! Hi, Kentucky!"

"Pug," he said. "Oh, you, Pug! My, but I'm glad to see you again, boy."

They talked quickly, telling in snatches what had happened to each since they separated, and both openly and whole-heartedly glad to be together again.

"I got a helmet, Kentuck," said Pug joyfully, and exhibited his German helmet with pride. "Tole you I'd get a good 'un, didn't I? An' I downed the cove that 'ad it meself. We potted at each other quite a bit—'im or me for it—an' I downed 'im, an' got 'is 'elmet."

Now the capture of the village was a notable feat of arms which was duly if somewhat briefly chronicled in the General Headquarters dispatch of the day with a line or two enumerating the depth and front of the advance made, the prisoners and material taken. The war correspondents have described the action more fully and in

100

more enthusiastic and picturesque language, and the action with notes of the number of shells fired, the battalions and batteries employed, and nice clear explanatory maps of the ground and dispositions of attackers and defenders will no doubt in due course occupy its proper place in the history of the war.

But none of these makes any mention of Pug and his helmet, although these apparently played quite an important part in the operation. Pug himself never understood his full share in it— remembered the whole affair as nothing but a horrible mix-up of noise, mud, bursting shells and drifting smoke, and his acquirement of a very fine helmet souvenir. Even when Pug told his story Kentucky hardly understood all it meant, only indeed came to realize it when he added to it those other official and semi-official accounts, his—Kentucky's—own experience, and the mysterious impulse that he had seen change the Anzacs' retreat into an attack, into the charge which swept up the Stonewalls and carried on into and over the village. To get the story complete as Kentucky came to piece it out and understand it we must go back and cover Pug's doings from the time Kentucky left him and the others in the shell-hole to carry the message back to the artillery F.O.O.

After the German counter-attack was caught in the nick of time and driven back with heavy loss, a good many of the counter-attackers instead of risking the run back to the shelter of their trench dropped into shell-holes and craters, and from here the more determined of them continued to shoot at any head showing in the British line. The men of the latter were also scattered along the broken ground in what at one time had been the open between two trenches, but was now a better position and in its innumerable deep shell craters offered better cover than the wrecked fragment of a trench behind them. On both sides too the gunners were ferociously strafing the opposition trenches, but since they dare not drop their shells too near to where they knew their own front lines to be located the tendency on both sides was for the front line to wriggle and crawl forward into the zone left uncovered by bursting high-explosive shells and shrapnel. The German and British infantry naturally did their best to discourage and make as expensive as possible the forward movement by the opposition, and industriously sniped with rifle and machine gun any men who exposed themselves for a moment. But when the counter-attack fell back Pug was for some minutes too busily engaged in helping to bandage up a badly wounded man to pay much attention to what the Germans were doing. When the job was completed he raised his head and looked out of the shell hole where he and the others were sheltering and peered round through the drifting smoke haze. He caught dim sight of some moving figures and raised his voice lustily. "Stretche-e-er!" he shouted, and after waiting a minute, again "Stre-tche-e-er!" Amidst all the uproar of battle it is not probable that his voice had a carrying power of more than scanty yards, but when no stretcher-bearers immediately materialized in answer to his call Pug appeared a good deal annoyed. "Wot d'you s'pose them blanky bearers is doin'?" he grumbled, then raised his voice and bawled again. He shouted and grumbled alternately for a few minutes with just the growing sense of annoyance that a man feels when he whistles for a taxi and no taxi appears. Two or three times he ducked instinctively at a hiss of a close bullet and once at the "Cr-r-ump" of a falling shell and the whistle of its flying splinters, and when he stood to shout he took care to keep well down in his shell hole, raising no more than his head above its level to allow his voice to carry above ground. Apparently, although he thought it unpleasantly risky to be above ground there, and in no way out of place for him not to expose himself, he took it quite for granted that stretcher-bearers would accept all the risk and come running to his bellowings. But in case it be thought that he expected too much, it ought to be remembered that it is the stretcher-bearers themselves who are responsible for such high expectations. Their salving of broken bodies from out the maelstrom of battle, their desperate rescues under fire, their readiness to risk the most appalling hazards, their indifference to wounds and death, their calm undertaking of impossibly difficult jobs, these very doings which by their constant performance have been reduced to no more than the normal, have come to be accepted as the matter-of-fact ordinary routine business of the stretcher-bearers. Pug, in fact, expected them to come when he called, only because he had seen them scores of times answer promptly to equally or even more risky calls.

And the stretcher-bearers in this instance did not fail him. A couple appeared looming hazily through the smoke, and at another call labored heavily over the broken ground to him. They saw the wounded man before Pug had time to make any explanation of his call, and without stopping to waste words, slid over the edge of the crater, dropped the stretcher in position beside the wounded man, ran a quick, workmanlike glance and touch over the first field-dressings on him, had him on the stretcher and hoisted up out of the hole all well inside a couple of minutes.

Pug returned to his own particular business, and settling himself against the sloping wall of the crater nearest the Germans took a cautious survey of the ground before him. At first he saw nothing but the rough, churned-up surface and a filmy curtain of smoke through which the resuming British bombardment was again beginning to splash fountains of shell-flung reek and dust. But as he looked a figure appeared, came forward at a scrambling run for a score of paces and dropped out of sight into some hole. At first sight of him Pug had instinctively thrust forward his rifle muzzle and snapped off a quick shot, but the man had run on apparently without taking any notice of it. Pug was a fair enough shot to feel some annoyance. "D'jer see that?" he asked his neighbor. "Beggar never even ducked; an' I'll bet I didn't go far off an inner on 'im." The neighbor was taking a long and careful sight over the edge of the pit. He fired, and without moving his rifle gazed earnestly in the direction he had shot. "Wot's that, Pug?" he said at last, jerking out the empty shell and reloading. "Who ducked? Ah, would yer!" he exclaimed hastily, and pumped out a rapid clipful of rounds. Pug joined in with a couple of shots and the dodging figures they had shot at vanished suddenly. "Wot's their game now, I wonder," said Pug. "D'you think they're edgin' in for another rush?" He had raised himself a little to look out, but the venomous hiss-zizz of a couple of bullets close past his head made him bob down hurriedly.

"You gotter look out," said the other man. "A lot o' blighters didn't bolt when we cut up their attack. They just dropped into any hole that come handy, an' they're lyin' there snipin' pot shots at any one that shows."

Pug banged off a shot, jerked the breech open and shut and banged off another. "See that," he said. "Same bloke I potted at afore. Not 'arf a cheeky blighter either. Keeps jumpin' up an' runnin' in to'ards us. But you wait till nex' time—I'll give 'im run." He settled himself nicely with elbow-rest, wide sprawled legs, and braced feet, and waited with careful eye on his sights and coiled finger about the trigger. Two minutes he waited, and then his rifle banged again, and he exclaimed delightedly, "I gottim, chum. I gottim that time. See 'im flop?" But his exclamation changed to one of angry disgust as he saw the man he supposed he had "got" rise from behind his cover, beckon vigorously to some one behind him, and move forward again another few steps.

Pug blazed another shot at him, and in response the man, in the very act of dropping to cover, stopped, straightened up, and after staring in Pug's direction for a moment, turned, and lifting the helmet from his head repeated the beckoning motion he had made before.

"Well of all the blinkin' cheek," said Pug wrathfully; "take that, you cow," firing again.

"Wot's up?" said his companion. "Is some bloke stringin' you?"

"Fair beats me," said the exasperated Pug. "I've 'ad half a dozen clean shots at 'im, an' 'e just laughs at 'em. But I've marked the last place 'e bogged down into, an' if 'e just pokes a nose out once more, 'e'll get it in the neck for keeps."

"Where is 'e?" said the interested chum; "show us, an' I'll drop it acrost 'im too when 'e pops out."

"No," said Pug firmly, "fair dinkum. 'E's my own private little lot, an' I'm goin' to see 'im safely 'ome myself. S-steady now, 'ere 'e comes again. Just 'avin' a look out, eh Fritz. Orright, m' son. Keep on lookin' an' it'll meet yer optic—plunk," and he fired. "Missed again," he said sadly as he saw a spurt of mud flick from the edge of the German's cover. "But lumme, chum, di'jer see the 'elmet that bloke 'ad?" The German it may be remembered had drawn attention to his helmet by taking it off and waving it, but Pug at that moment had been too exasperated by the impudence of the man's exposure to notice the helmet. But this time a gleam of light caught the heavy metal "chin-strap" that hung from it, and although the helmet itself was covered with the usual service cover of gray cloth, Pug could see distinctly that it was one of the old pickel-hauben type—one of the kind he so greatly coveted as a "souvenir."

"That settles it," said Pug firmly. "I'm goin' to lay for that bloke till I gets 'im, an' then when we advance I'll 'ave 'is 'elmet."

He lay for several minutes, watching the spot where the German was concealed as a cat watches a mouse-hole, and when his patience was rewarded by a glimpse of gray uniform he took steady aim, carefully squeezed the trigger until he felt the faint check of its second pull-off, held his breath, and gave the final squeeze, all in exact accordance with the school of musketry instructions. The patch of gray vanished, and Pug could not tell whether he had scored a hit, but almost immediately he saw the spike and rounded

104

top of the helmet lift cautiously into sight. Again Pug took slow and deliberate aim but then hesitated, "Tchick-tchicked" softly between his teeth, aimed again and fired. The helmet vanished with a jerk. "Lookin' over the edge of 'is 'ole, 'e was," said Pug. "An' at first I didn't like to shoot for fear of spoilin' that 'elmet. But arter all," he conceded cheerfully, "I dunno' that it wouldn't maybe improve it as a fust-class sooven-eer to 'ave a neat little three-oh-three 'ole drilled in it."

"Did you drill it?" asked his companion directly.

"Dunno," admitted Pug, "but I'm keepin' a careful eye on 'im, an' I'll soon know if 'e moves again."

But in the process of keeping a careful eye Pug was tempted for an instant into keeping a less careful head under cover than the situation demanded. A bullet leaped whutt past within an inch of his ear and he dropped flat to earth with an oath. "That was 'im," he said, "I saw the flash of 'is rifle. Looks like 'e's got me piped off, an' it's goin' to be 'im or me for it."

Chick and another man in the same hole had been busy shooting at any mark that presented, but when their every appearance above ground began to be greeted by an unpleasantly close bullet, they ceased to fire and squatted back in the hole to watch Pug and the conducting of his duel. A dozen times he and the German fired, each drawing or returning instant shot for shot, Pug moving from one spot to another in the shell crater, pushing his rifle out slowly, lifting his head cautiously an inch at a time.

Over their heads the great shells shrieked and rushed, round them crackled a spattering rifle fire, the occasional hammering of a machine gun, the rolling crash and whirr of bursting shells and flying splinters. Wide out to right and left of them, far to their front and rear the roar of battle ran, long-thundering and unbroken, in a deafening chorus of bellowing guns, the vibrating rattle of rifles and machine guns, the sharp detonations and reports of shells and bombs and grenades. But Pug and, in lesser degree, his companions, were quite heedless of all these things, of how the battle moved or stayed still. For them the struggle had boiled down into the solitary duel between Pug and his German; the larger issues were for the moment completely overshadowed, as in war they so often are, by the mere individual and personal ones. Pug insisted in finishing off his duel single-handed, declining to have the others

105

there interfere in it. "It's 'im or me for it," he repeated, "fair dinkum. An' I'm goin' to get 'im and 'is 'elmet on my blinkin' own."

He decided at last to move his position, to crawl along and try to catch his opponent in flank, to stalk his enemy as a hunter stalks a hidden buck. Since he could not escape from the crater they were in without exposing himself to that watchful rifle, he scraped down with his entrenching tool a couple of feet of the rim of the crater where it formed a wall dividing off another crater. When he had cleared the passage he came back and fired another shot, just to keep his enemy watching in the same spot for him, and hurriedly crawled over into the next crater, squirmed and wriggled away from it along cracks and holes and folds of the torn and tumbled ground in a direction that he reckoned would allow him to reach the German sheltering in his hole and behind a broken hillock of earth. But before he reached such a position as he desired he found himself looking over into a deep crater occupied by an officer and half a dozen men with a machine gun.

The officer looked up and caught sight of him. "Hullo, Sneath," he said. "Where are you off to? You're moving the wrong way, aren't you? The order was to retire, and you're moving forward."

Pug wriggled over into the crater and crouched puffing and blowing for a moment. "I 'adn't 'eard nothin' about retiring, sir," he said doubtfully.

"That's the order," said the officer briskly. "I don't know what it means any more than you do, but there it is. You'd better wait now and move back with us."

Pug was annoyed—exceedingly annoyed. This retirement looked like losing him his duel, and what was more, losing him his coveted helmet. Retirement was a thing he had not for an instant calculated upon. He had taken it quite for granted that if he could slay the wearer of the helmet, the helmet was his, that he had only to wait until the line advanced to go straight to it and pick it up. With a vague idea that he would have managed the affair much better on his own, without these interfering directions of his movements, he began to wish he had never come across this officer, and from that passed to wondering whether he couldn't give the officer the slip and finish off his program in his own way.

At that moment the British artillery fire redoubled in intensity and the rush of shells overhead rose to a roaring gale.

"Sharp there," said the officer. "Get that gun picked up. Now's our chance to get back while the guns are socking it into 'em."

He was right, of course, and their chances of retirement were likely to be improved by the heavier covering fire. Pug was also right in a half-formed idea that had come to him—that the covering fire would also lessen the risk of a move forward, or as he put it to himself— "With all them shells about their ears they'll be too busy keepin' their heads down to do much shootin' at me if I chance a quick rush; an' most likely I'd be on top o' that bloke wi' the 'elmet afore 'e knew it."

The others were picking up the machine gun and preparing to move, and Pug took a long and careful look over the edge of the hole to locate his helmet wearer. With a quick exclamation he snatched the rifle to his shoulder, aimed, and fired.

"That'll do," said the officer sharply turning at the sound of the shot. "Cease firing and get along back." But Pug was gazing hard in the direction of his shot. "I've got 'im," he said triumphantly, "I'll swear I got 'im that time. Showin' a fair mark 'e was, an' I saw 'im jerk 'an roll when I fired."

"Never mind that," said the officer impatiently. "There's their rifle fire beginning again. Time we were out of this. Keep down as well as you can all of you. Move yourselves now."

The men began to scramble out of the hole, and in an instant Pug's mind was made up. They were retiring; so far as he knew the battalion might be retiring out of the line, out of the battle, and out of the reach of chances of German helmets. And meantime there was his helmet lying there waiting to be picked up, lying within a hundred yards of him.

He climbed up the rear wall of the crater, halted and spoke hurriedly to the officer. "I won't be 'alf a mo', sir," he said. "Something there I want to pick up an' bring in," and without waiting for any reply turned and bolted across the open towards his helmet. The officer was consumed with a quick gust of anger at such disobedience. "Here," he shouted and scrambled out of the pit. "Hi, come back you"; and as Pug gave no sign of having heard him, he shouted again and ran a few paces after him.

And so it was that about a dozen Anzacs rising sullenly and

grumblingly out of a big shell crater in reluctant obedience to the order to retire, saw a khaki figure rise into sight and go charging straight forward towards the enemy, and a second later the figure of an officer bound into sight and follow him.

Two or three of the Anzacs voiced together the thought that rose to all their minds.

"Who said retire.... What blundering fool twisted the order ... retire, Gostrewth, they're advancing ... us retire, an' them goin' forward ..."

To them the position required little thinking over. They could see some men advancing, and distinctly see an officer too at that. And how many more the smoke hid——

In an instant they were swarming up and out of their crater; there was a wild yell, a shrill "Cooee," a confused shouting, "Come on, boys ... at 'em, Anzacs ... Advance, Australia," and the dozen went plunging off forward. Out to right and left of them the yell ran like fire through dry grass, the coo-ees rose long and shrill; as if by magic the dead ground sprouted gleaming bayonets and scrambling khaki figures. Every man who looked saw a ragged and swiftly growing line surging forward, and every man, asking nothing more, taking only this plain evidence of advance, made haste—exactly as Kentucky's companions made haste—to fling into it. Straight at the flashing rifles and the drifting fog-bank of shell smoke that marked the German position the shifting wave swept and surged, the men yelling, shouting and cheering. Bullets beating down upon them, shells crumpling and smashing amongst them cut them down by dozens, but neither halted nor slowed down the charging line. It poured on, flooded in over the wrecked trenches and dug-outs, the confused litter of shell holes big and little, piled earth heaps, occasional fragments of brickwork and splintered beams that alone remained of the village. The flank attacks that had been launched a few minutes before and held up staggering under the ferocious fire that met them, found the weight of their opposition suddenly grow less, took fresh breath and thrust fiercely in again, gained a footing, felt the resistance weaken and bend and break, and in a moment were through and into the tumbled wreckage of a defense, shooting and stabbing and bayoneting, bombing the dug-outs, rounding up the prisoners, pushing on until they came in touch with the swirling edges of the frontal attack's wave, and joining them turned and overran the last struggling remnants of the defense. The village was taken; the line pushed out beyond it, took firm grip of a fresh patch of ground, spread swiftly and linked up with the attack that raged on out to either side and bit savagely into the crumbling German line.

These wider issues were of course quite beyond the knowledge or understanding of Pug. He had come uninjured to the spot where his German lay, found he was an officer and quite dead, snatched up the helmet that lay beside him, and turned to hurry back. Only then was he aware of the line charging and barging down upon him, and understanding nothing of why or how it had come there, noticing only from a glimpse of some faces he knew that men of his own battalion were in it, he slipped his arm through the chinstrap of his captured helmet, turned again and ran forward with the rest. With them he played his part in the final overrunning of the village—the usual confused, scuffling jumble of a part played by the average infantry private in an attack, a nightmarish mixture of noise and yelling, of banging rifles, shattering bomb reports, a great deal of smoke, the whistle of passing bullets, the crackling snap and smack of their striking ground and stone, swift appearance and disappearance of running figures. He had a momentary vision of men grouped about a black dug-out mouth hurling grenades down it; joined a wild rush with several others on a group of gray-coated Germans who stood firm even to a bayonet finish. Scrambling and scuffling down and up the steep sides of the smaller shell craters, round the slippery crumbling edges of the larger, he caught glimpses—this towards the end—of scattered groups or trickling lines of white-faced prisoners with long gray coats flapping about their ankles, and hands held high over their heads, being shepherded out towards the British lines by one or two guards. All these scattered impressions were linked up by many panting, breathless scrambles over a chaos of torn and broken ground pocked and pitted with the shell craters set as close as the cells of a broken honeycomb, and ended with a narrow escape, averted just in time by one of his officers, from firing upon a group of men—part of the flank attack as it proved—who appeared mysteriously out of the smoke where Germans had been firing and throwing stick-grenades a moment before.

Through all the turmoil Pug clung tightly to his helmet. He knew that there had been a stiff fight and that they had won, was vaguely pleased at the comforting fact, and much more distinctly pleased and satisfied with the possession of his souvenir. He took the first opportunity when the line paused and proceeded to sort itself out beyond the village, to strip the cloth off his prize and examine it. It was an officer's pickelhaube, resplendent in all its glory of glistening black patent-leather, gleaming brass eagle spread-winged across its front, fierce spike on top and heavy-linked chain "chin-strap" of shining brass. Pug was hugely pleased with his trophy, displayed it pridefully and told briefly the tale of his duel with the late owner. He told nothing of how the securing of his prize had assisted at the taking of the village, for the good reason that he himself did not know it, and up to then in fact did not even know that they had taken a village.

He tied the helmet securely to his belt with a twisted bit of wire, and at the urgent command of a sweating and mud-bedaubed sergeant prepared to dig. "Are we stoppin' 'ere then?" he stayed to ask.

"Suppose so," said the sergeant, "seeing we've taken our objective and got this village."

Pug gaped at him, and then looked round wonderingly at the tossed and tumbled shell-riddled chaos of shattered earth that was spread about them. "Got this village," he said. "Lumme, where's the village then?"

Another man there laughed at him. "You came over the top o' it, Pug," he said. "Don't you remember the broken beam you near fell over, back there a piece? That was a bit o' one o' the houses in the village. An' d'you see that little bit o' gray wall there? That's some more o' the village."

Pug looked hard at it. "An' that's the village, is it," he said cheerfully. "Lor' now, I might 'ave trod right on top o' it by accident, or even tripped over it, if it 'ad been a bit bigger village. You can keep it; I'd rather 'ave my 'elmet."

CHAPTER XIII

WITH THE TANKS

Soon after Kentucky rejoined them the Stonewalls were moved forward a little clear of the village they had helped to take, just as one or two heavy shells whooped over from the German guns and dropped crashing on the ground that had been theirs. The men were spread out along shell holes and told to dig in for better cover because a bit of a redoubt on the left flank hadn't been taken and bullets were falling in enfilade from it.

"Dig, you cripples," said the sergeant, "dig in. Can't you see that if they counter-attack from the front now you'll get shot in the back while you're lining the front edge of those shell holes. Get to it there, you Pug."

"Shot in the back, linin' the front," said Pug as the sergeant passed on. "Is it a conundrum, Kentuck?"

"Sounds sort of mixed," admitted Kentucky. "But it's tainted some with the truth. That redoubt is half rear to us. If another lot comes at us in front and we get up on the front edge of this shell hole, there's nothing to stop the redoubt bullets hitting us in the back. Look at that," he concluded, nodding upward to where a bullet had smacked noisily into the mud above their heads as they squatted in the hole.

The two commenced wearily to cut out with their trenching tools a couple of niches in the sides of the crater which would give them

111

protection from the flank and rear bullets. They made reasonably secure cover and then stayed to watch a hurricane bombardment that was developing on the redoubt. "Goo on the guns," said Pug joyfully. "That's the talk; smack 'em about."

The gunners "smacked 'em about" with fifteen savage minutes' deluge of light and heavy shells, blotting out the redoubt in a whirlwind of fire-flashes, belching smoke clouds and dust haze. Then suddenly the tempest ceased to play there, lifted and shifted and fell roaring in a wall of fire and steel beyond the low slope which the redoubt crowned.

With past knowledge of what the lift and the further barrage meant the two men in the shell-pit turned and craned their necks and looked out along the line.

"There they go," said Pug suddenly, and "Attacking round a half-circle," said Kentucky. The British line was curved in a horse-shoe shape about the redoubt and the two being out near one of the points could look back and watch clearly the infantry attack launching from the center and half-way round the sides of the horse-shoe. They saw the khaki figures running heavily, scrambling round and through the scattered shell holes, and presently, as a crackle of rifle fire rose and rose and swelled to a sullen roar with the quick, rhythmic clatter of machine guns beating through it, they saw also the figures stumbling and falling, the line thinning and shredding out and wasting away under the withering fire.

The sergeant dodged along the pit-edge above them. "Covering fire," he shouted, "at four hundred—slam it in," and disappeared. The two opened fire, aiming at the crest of the slope and beyond the tangle of barbed wire which alone indicated the position of the redoubt.

They only ceased to fire when they saw the advanced fringe of the line, of a line by now woefully thinned and weakened, come to the edge of the barbed wire and try to force a way through it.

"They're beat," gasped Pug. "They're done in ..." and cursed long and bitterly, fingering nervously at his rifle the while. "Time we rung in again," said Kentucky. "Aim steady and pitch 'em well clear of the wire." The two opened careful fire again while the broken remnants of the attacking line ran and hobbled and crawled back or into the cover of shell holes. A second wave flooded out in a new assault, but by now the German artillery joining in helped it and the new line was cut down, broken and beaten back before it had covered half the distance to the entanglements. Kentucky and Pug and others of the Stonewalls near them could only curse helplessly as they watched the tragedy and plied their rifles in a slender hope of some of their bullets finding those unseen loopholes and embrasures.

"An' wot's the next item o' the program, I wonder?" said Pug half an hour after the last attack had failed, half an hour filled with a little shooting, a good deal of listening to the pipe and whistle of overhead bullets and the rolling thunder of the guns, a watching of the shells falling and spouting earth and smoke on the defiant redoubt.

"Reinforcements and another butt-in at it, I expect," surmised Kentucky. "Don't see anything else for it. Looks like this pimple-on-the-map of a redoubt was holdin' up any advance on this front. Anyhow I'm not hankering to go pushin' on with that redoubt bunch shootin' holes in my back, which they'd surely do."

"Wot's all the buzz about be'ind us?" said Pug suddenly, raising himself for a quick look over the covering edge of earth behind him, and in the act of dropping again stopped and stared with raised eyebrows and gaping mouth.

"What is it?" said Kentucky quickly, and also rose, and also stayed risen and staring in amazement. Towards them, lumbering and rolling, dipping heavily into the shell holes, heaving clumsily out of them, moving with a motion something between that of a half-sunken ship and a hamstrung toad, striped and banded and splashed from head to foot, or, if you prefer it, from fo'c'sl-head to cutwater, with splashes of lurid color, came His Majesty's Land Ship "Here We Are."

"Gor-strewth!" ejaculated Pug. "Wha-what is it?"

Kentucky only gasped.

"'Ere," said Pug hurriedly, "let's gerrout o' this. It's comin' over atop of us," and he commenced to scramble clear.

But a light of understanding was dawning on Kentucky's face and a wide grin growing on his lips. "It's one of the Tanks," he said, and giggled aloud as the Here We Are dipped her nose and slid head first into a huge shell crater in ludicrous likeness to a squat bull-pup sitting back on its haunches and dragged into a hole: "I've heard lots about 'em, but the seein' beats all the hearin' by whole streets," and he and Pug laughed aloud together as the Here We Are's face and gun-port eyes and bent-elbow driving gear appeared above the crater rim in still more ridiculous resemblance to an amazed toad emerging from a rain-barrel. The creature lumbered past them, taking in its stride the narrow trench dug to link up the shell holes, and the laughter on Kentucky's lips died to thoughtfully serious lines as his eye caught the glint of fat, vicious-looking gun muzzles peering from their ports.

"Haw haw haw," guffawed Pug as the monster lurched drunkenly, checked and steadied itself with one foot poised over a deep hole, halted and backed away, and edged nervously round the rim of the hole. "See them machine guns pokin' out, Kentucky," he continued delightedly. "They won't 'arf pepper them Huns when they gets near enough."

Fifty yards in the wake of the Here We Are a line of men followed up until an officer halted them along the front line where Pug and Kentucky were posted.

"You blokes just takin' 'im out for an airin'?" Pug asked one of the newcomers. "Oughtn't you to 'ave 'im on a leadin' string?"

"Here we are, Here we are again," chanted the other and giggled spasmodically. "An' ain't he just hot stuff! But wait till you see 'im get to work with his sprinklers."

"Does 'e bite?" asked Pug, grinning joyously. "Oughtn't you to 'ave 'is muzzle on?"

"Bite," retorted another. "He's a bloomin' Hun-eater. Jes' gulps 'em whole, coal-scuttle 'ats an' all."

"He's a taed," said another. "A lollopin, flat-nosed, splay-fittit, ugly puddock, wi's hin' legs stuck oot whaur his front should be."

"Look at 'im, oh look at 'im ... he's alive, lad, nobbut alive." ... "Does every bloomin' thing but talk." ... "Skatin' he is now, skatin' on 'is off hind leg," came a chorus of delighted comment.

"Is he goin' to waltz in and take that redoubt on his ownsum?" asked

114

Kentucky. "No," some one told him. "We give him ten minutes' start and then follow on and pick up the pieces, and the prisoners."

They lay there laughing and joking and watching the uncouth antics of the monster waddling across the shell-riddled, ground, cheering when it appeared to trip and recover itself, cheering when it floundered sideways into a hole and crawled out again, cheering most wildly of all when it reached the barbed-wire entanglements, waddled through, bursting them apart and trailing them in long tangles behind it, or trampling them calmly under its churning caterpillar-wheel-bands. It was little wonder they cheered and less wonder they laughed. The Here We Are's motions were so weirdly alive and life-like, so playfully ponderous, so massively ridiculous, that it belonged by nature to nothing outside a Drury Lane Panto. At one moment it looked exactly like a squat tug-boat in a heavy cross sea or an ugly tide-rip, lurching, dipping, rolling rail and rail, plunging wildly bows under, tossing its nose up and squattering again stern-rail deep, pitching and heaving and diving and staggering, but always pushing forward. Next minute it was a monster out of Prehistoric Peeps, or a new patent fire-breathing dragon from the pages of a very Grimm Fairy Tale, nosing its way blindly over the Fairy Prince's pitfalls; next it was a big broad-buttocked sow nuzzling and rooting as it went; next it was a drunk man reeling and staggering, rolling and falling, scrabbling and crawling; next it was—was anything on or in, or underneath the earth, anything at all except a deadly, grim, purposeful murdering product of modern war.

The infantry pushed out after it when it reached the barbed wire, and although they took little heed to keep cover—being much more concerned not to miss any of the grave and comic antics of their giant joke than to shelter from flying bullets—the line went on almost without casualties. "Mighty few bullets about this time," remarked Kentucky, who with Pug had moved out along with the others "to see the fun." "That's 'cos they're too busy with the old Pepper-pots, an' the Pepper-pots is too busy wi' them to leave much time for shootin' at us," said Pug gayly. It was true too. The Pepper-pots—a second one had lumbered into sight from the center of the horseshoe curve—were drawing a tearing hurricane of machine-gun bullets that beat and rattled on their armored sides like hail on a window-pane. They waddled indifferently through the storm and Here We Are, crawling carefully across a trench, halted half-way over and sprinkled bullets up and down its length to port and starboard for a minute, hitched itself over, steered straight for a fire-streaming machine-gun embrasure. It squirted a jet of lead into the loophole, walked on, butted at the emplacement once or twice, got a grip of it under the upward sloped caterpillar band, climbed jerkily till it stood reared up on end like a frightened colt, ground its driving bands round and round, and—fell forward on its face with a cloud of dust belching up and out from the collapsed dug-out. Then it crawled out of the wreckage, crunching over splintered beams and broken concrete, wheeled and cruised casually down the length of a crooked trench, halting every now and then to spray bullets on any German who showed or to hail a stream of them down the black entrance to a dug-out, straying aside to nose over any suspicions cranny, swinging round again to plod up the slope in search of more trenches.

The infantry followed up, cheering and laughing like children at a fair, rounding up batches of prisoners who crawled white-faced and with scared eyes from dug-out doors and trench corners, shouting jests and comments at the lumbering Pepper-pots.

A yell went up as the Here We Are, edging along a trench, lurched suddenly, staggered, sideslipped, and half disappeared in a fog of dust. The infantry raced up and found it with its starboard driving gear grinding and churning full power and speed of revolution above ground and the whole port side and gear down somewhere in the depths of the collapsed trench, grating and squealing and flinging out clods of earth as big as clothes-baskets. Then the engines eased, slowed, and stopped, and after a little and in answer to the encouraging yells of the men outside, a scuttle jerked open and a grimy figure crawled out.

"Blimey," said Pug rapturously, "'ere's Jonah 'isself. Ol' Pepper-pot's spewed 'im out."

But "Jonah" addressed himself pointedly and at some length to the laughing spectators, and they, urged on by a stream of objurgation and invective, fell to work with trenching-tools, with spades retrieved from the trench, with bare hands and busy fingers, to break down the trench-side under Here We Are's starboard driver, and pile it down into the trench and under the uplifted end of her port one. The second Pepper-pot cruised up and brought to adjacent to the operations with a watchful eye on the horizon. It was well she did, for suddenly a crowd of Germans seeing or sensing that one of the monsters was out of action, swarmed out of cover on the crest

116

and came storming down on the party. Here We Are could do nothing; but the sister ship could, and did, do quite a lot to those Germans. It sidled round so as to bring both bow guns and all its broadside to bear and let loose a close-quarter tornado of bullets that cut the attackers to rags. The men who had ceased digging to grab their rifles had not time to fire a shot before the affair was over and "Jonah" was again urging them to their spade-work. Then when he thought the way ready, Here We Are at his orders steamed ahead again, its lower port side scraping and jarring along the trench wall, the drivers biting and gripping at the soft ground. Jerkily, a foot at a time, it scuffled its way along the trench till it came to a sharp angle of it where a big shell hole had broken down the wall. But just as the starboard driver was reaching out over the shell hole and the easy job of plunging into it, gaining a level keel and climbing out the other side, the trench wall on the right gave way and the Here We Are sank its starboard side level to and then below the port one. She had fallen bodily into a German dug-out, but after a pause to regain its shaken breath—or the crew's—it began once more to revolve its drivers slowly, and to churn out behind them, first a cloud of dust and clots of earth, then, as the starboard driver bit deeper into the dug-out, a mangled débris of clothing and trench-made furniture. On the ground above the infantry stood shrieking with laughter, while the frantic skipper raved unheard-of oaths and the Here We Are pawed out and hoofed behind, or caught on its driving band and hoisted in turn into the naked light of day, a splintered bedstead, a chewed up blanket or two, separately and severally the legs, back, and seat of a red velvet arm-chair, a torn gray coat and a forlorn and muddy pair of pink pajama trousers tangled up in one officer's field boot. And when the drivers got their grip again and the Here We Are rolled majestically forward and up the further sloping side of the shell crater and halted to take the skipper aboard again, Pug dragged a long branch from the fascines in the trench débris, slid it up one leg and down the other of the pink pajamas, tied the boot by its laces to the tip and jammed the root into a convenient crevice in the Tank's stern. And so beflagged she rolled her triumphant way up over the captured redoubt and down the other side, with the boot-tip bobbing and swaying and jerking at the end of her pink tail. The sequel to her story may be told here, although it only came back to the men who decorated her after filtering round the firing line, up and down the communication lines, round half the hospitals and most of the messes at or behind the Front.

And many as came to be the Tales of the Tanks, this of the Pink-

Tailed 'un, as Pug called her, belonged unmistakably to her and, being so, was joyfully recognized and acclaimed by her decorators. She came in due time across the redoubt, says the story, and bore down on the British line at the other extreme of the horseshoe to where a certain infantry C.O., famed in past days for a somewhat speedy and hectic career, glared in amazement at the apparition lurching and bobbing and bowing and crawling toad-like towards him.

"I knew," he is reported to have afterwards admitted, "I knew it couldn't be that I'd got 'em again. But in the old days I always had one infallible sign. Crimson rats and purple snakes I might get over; but if they had pink tails, I knew I was in for it certain. And I tell you it gave me quite a turn to see this blighter waddling up and wagging the old pink tail."

But this end of the story only came to the Stonewalls long enough after—just as it is said to have come in time to the ears of the Here We Are's skipper, and, mightily pleasing him and his crew, set him chuckling delightedly and swearing he meant to apply and in due and formal course obtain permission to change his land-ship's name, and having regretfully parted with the pink tail, immortalize it in the name of H.M.L.S. The D.T.'s.

CHAPTER XIV

THE BATTLE HYMN

Kentucky was suddenly aware of an overpowering thirst. Pug being appealed to shook his empty water-bottle in reply. "But I'll soon get some," he said cheerfully and proceeded to search amongst the German dead lying thick around them. He came back with a full water-bottle and a haversack containing sausage and dark brown bread, and the two squatted in a shell hole and made a good meal of the dead man's rations. They felt a good deal the better of it, and the expectation of an early move back out of the firing line completed their satisfaction. The Stonewalls would be relieved presently, they assured each other; had been told their bit was done when the village was taken; and that was done and the redoubt on top of it. They weren't sure how many Stonewalls had followed on in the wake of the tank, but they'd all be called back soon, and the two agreed cordially that they wouldn't be a little bit sorry to be out of this mud and murder game for a spell.

An attempt was made after a little to sort out the confusion of units that had resulted from the advance, the Stonewalls being collected together as far as possible, and odd bunches of Anzacs and Highlanders and Fusiliers sent off in the direction of their appointed rallying-places. The work was made more difficult by the recommencing of a slow and methodical bombardment by the German guns and the reluctance of the men to move from their cover for no other purpose than to go and find cover again in another part of the line. Scattered amongst craters and broken trenches as the Stonewalls were, even after they were more or less collected together, it was hard to make any real estimate of the casualties, and yet it was plain enough to all that the battalion had lost heavily. As odd men and groups dribbled in, Kentucky and Pug questioned them eagerly for any news of Larry, and at last heard a confused story from a stretcher-bearer of a party of Stonewalls that had been cut off, had held a portion of trench against a German bombing attack, and had been wiped out in process of the defense. Larry, their informant was almost sure, was one of the casualties, but he could not say whether killed, slightly or seriously wounded.

"Wish I knowed 'e wasn't hurt too bad," said Pug. "Rotten luck if 'e is."

"Anyhow," said Kentucky, "we two have been mighty lucky to come through it all so far, with nothing more than your arm scratch between us."

"Touch wood," said Pug warningly. "Don't go boastin' without touchin' wood."

Kentucky, who stood smoking with his hands buried deep in his pockets, laughed at his earnest tone. But his laugh died, and he and Pug glanced up apprehensively as they heard the thin, distant wail of an approaching shell change and deepen to the roaring tempest of heart and soul-shaking noise that means a dangerously close burst.

"Down, Pug," cried Kentucky sharply, and on the same instant both flung themselves flat in the bottom of their shelter. Both felt and heard the rending concussion, the shattering crash of the burst, were sensible of the stunning shock, a sensation of hurtling and falling, of ... empty blackness and nothingness.

Kentucky recovered himself first. He felt numbed all over except in his left side and arm, which pricked sharply and pulsed with pain at a movement. He opened his eyes slowly with a vague idea that he had been lying there for hours, and it was with intense amazement that he saw the black smoke of the burst still writhing and thinning against the sky, heard voices calling and asking was any one hurt, who was hit, did it catch any one. He called an answer feebly at first, then more strongly, and then as memory came back with a rush, loud and sharp, "Pug! are you there, Pug? Pug!" One or two men came groping and fumbling to him through the smoke, but he would not let them lift or touch him until they had searched for Pug. "He was just beside me," he said eagerly. "He can't be hurt badly. Do hunt for him, boys. It's poor old Pug. Oh, Pug!"

"H'lo, Kentuck ... you there?" came feebly back. With a wrench Kentucky was on his knees, staggered to his feet, and running to the voice. "Pug," he said, stooping over the huddled figure. "You're not hurt bad, are you, Pug, boy?" With clothing torn to rags, smeared and dripping with blood, with one leg twisted horribly under him, with a red cut gaping deep over one eye, Pug looked up and grinned weakly. "Orright," he said; "I'm ... orright. But I tole you, Kentuck ... I tole you to touch wood."

A couple of stretcher-bearers hurried along, and when the damages were assessed it was found that Pug was badly hurt, with one leg smashed, with a score of minor wounds, of which one in the side and one in the breast might be serious. Kentucky had a broken hand, torn arm, lacerated shoulder, and a heavily bruised set of ribs. So Pug was lifted on to a stretcher, and Kentucky, asserting stoutly that he could walk and that there was no need to waste a precious stretcher on carrying him, had his wounds bandaged and started out alongside the bearers who carried Pug. The going was bad, and the unavoidable jolting and jerking as the bearers stumbled over the rough ground must have been sheer agony to the man on the stretcher. But no groan or whimper came from Pug's tight lips, that he opened only to encourage Kentucky to keep on, to tell him it wouldn't be far now, to ask the bearers to go slow to give Kentucky a chance to keep up. But it was no time or place to go slow. The shells were still screaming and bursting over and about the ground they were crossing, gusts of rifle bullets or lonely whimpering ones still whistled and hummed past. A fold in the ground brought them cover presently from the bullets, but not from the shells, and the bearers pushed doggedly on. Kentucky kept up with difficulty, for he was feeling weak and spent, and it was with a sigh of relief that he saw the bearers halt and put the stretcher down. "How do you feel, Pug?" he asked. "Bit sore," said Pug with sturdy cheerfulness. "But it's nothin' too bad. But I wish we was outer this. We both got Blighty ones, Kentuck, an' we'll go 'ome together. Now we're on the way 'ome, I'd hate to have another of them shells drop on us, and put us out for good, mebbe."

They pushed on again, for the light was failing, and although the moon was already up, the half-light made the broken ground more difficult than ever to traverse. Pug had fallen silent, and one of the

121

bearers, noticing the gripped lips and pain-twisted face, called to the other man and put the stretcher down and fumbled out a pill. "Swallow that," he said, and put it between Pug's lips; "an' that's the last one I have." He daubed a ghastly blue cross on Pug's cheek to show he had been given an opiate, and then they went on again.

They crept slowly across the ground where the Germans had made one of their counter-attacks, and the price they had paid in it was plain to be seen in the piled heaps of dead that lay sprawled on the open and huddled anyhow in the holes and ditches. There were hundreds upon hundreds in that one patch of ground alone, and Kentucky wondered vaguely how many such patches there were throughout the battlefield. The stretcher-bearers were busy with the wounded, who in places still remained with the dead, and sound German prisoners under ridiculously slender guards were carrying in stretchers with badly wounded Germans or helping less severely wounded ones to walk back to the British rear. A little further on they crossed what had been a portion of trench held by the Germans and from which they appeared to have been driven by shell and mortar fire. Here there were no wounded, and of the many dead the most had been literally blown to pieces, or, flung bodily from their shelters, lay broken and buried under tumbled heaps of earth. Half a dozen Germans in long, flapping coats and heavy steel "coal-scuttle" helmets worked silently, searching the gruesome débris for any living wounded; and beyond them stood a solitary British soldier on guard over them, leaning on his bayoneted rifle and watching them. Far to the rear the flashes of the British guns lit the darkening sky with vivid, flickering gleams that came and went incessantly, like the play of summer lightning. It brought to Kentucky, trudging beside the stretcher, the swift memory of lines from a great poem that he had learned as a child and long since forgotten—the Battle Hymn of his own country. In his mind he quoted them now with sudden realization of the exactness of their fitting to the scene before him—"Mine eyes have seen the glory of the coming of the Lord, He is trampling out the vintage where the grapes of wrath are stored, He hath loosed the fateful lightning of His terrible swift sword; His truth is marching on." Here surely in these broken dead, in the silent, dejected prisoners, in the very earth she had seized and that now had been wrested from her, was Germany's vintage, the tramplings out of the grapes of a wrath long stored, the smitten of the swift sword that flashed unloosed at last in the gun-fire lightning at play across the sky.

For the rest of the way that he walked back to the First Aid Post the words of the verse kept running over in his pain-numbed and weary mind—"... where the grapes of wrath are stored; trampling out the vintage where the grapes of wrath ..." over and over again.

And when at last they came to the trench that led to the underground dressing-station just as the guns had waked again to a fresh spasm of fury that set the sky ablaze with their flashes and the air roaring to their deep, rolling thunders, Kentucky's mind went back to where the great shells would be falling, pictured to him the flaming fires, the rending, shattering crashes, the tearing whirlwinds of destruction, that would be devastating the German lines. "Grapes of wrath," he whispered. "God, yes—bitter grapes of wrath." And in his fancy the guns caught up the word from his mouth, and tossed it shouting in long-drawn, shaking thunder: "Wrath—wrath—wrath!"

CHAPTER XV

CASUALTIES

A deep and comparatively uninjured German dug-out had been adapted for use as a dressing-station. Its entrance lay in a little cup-shaped depression with a steep, sloping bank behind it, and the position of this bank and the entrance opening out of it away from the British lines had probably been the saving of it from shell fire. Kentucky groped his way down the dark stairway, and the bearers followed with Pug on the stretcher. The stair was horribly steep, built in high and narrow wooden steps which were coated with thick, slippery mud, and it was with some difficulty that the stretcher was brought down. The stair opened out direct into a large, well-built dug-out with planked floor, walls and roof, and beyond it again a narrow passage led to a further room, also well built and plank lined, but much longer, and so narrow that it barely gave room for men to be laid across it. This chamber, too, was filled with wounded, some of them stretched at full length, others squatting close packed about the floor. The first room was used by the doctors, because, being more widely built, it gave room for a couple of tables. There were three doctors there, two working at the tables, the third amongst the cases huddled along the wall. Kentucky took his place, leaning back against the wall and waiting his turn, but Pug was carried almost at once to one of the tables.

"Have you heard anything about how the whole show is going?" Kentucky asked one of the orderlies. "Not a word," said the man. "Leastways, we've heard so many words you can't believe any of 'em. Some o' the casualties tells us one thing an' some another. But we've bumped the Hun back a lump, that's sure. They all tell us that."

Kentucky stayed there some minutes longer, waiting his turn and watching the doctors at their work. They were kept hard at it. The casualties came stumbling down the stair in an unbroken procession, and in turn passed along to the doctors at the tables. Most of those that walked had bandages about their heads, faces, hands, or arms; most of them were smeared and spattered with blood, all of them were plastered thick with mud. Many had sleeves slit open or shirts cut away, and jackets slung loosely over their shoulders, and as they moved glimpses of white flesh and patches of bandage showed vividly fresh and clean behind the torn covering of blood-stained and muddy khaki. As fast as the doctor finished one man another took his place, and without an instant's pause the doctor washed from his mind the effort of thought concentrated on the last case, pounced on the newcomer, and, hurriedly stripping off the bandages, plunged into the problem of the fresh case, examining, diagnosing, and labeling it, cleansing the wound of the clotted blood and mud that clung about it, redressing and bandaging it. Then each man's breast was bared and a hypodermic injection of "anti-tetanus" serum made, and the man passed along to join the others waiting to go back to the ambulances. And before he was well clear of the table the doctor had turned and was busied about the next case. The work went on at top speed, as smooth as sweet-running machinery, as fast and efficiently as the sorting and packing of goods in a warehouse by a well-drilled and expert staff. It was curiously like the handling of merchandise, if you gave your main attention to the figures passing down the stairs, moving into line up to the tables, halting there a few minutes, moving on again and away. The men might have been parcels shifting one by one up to the packers' tables and away from them, or those pieces of metal in a factory which trickle up leisurely to a whirling lathe, are seized by it, turned, poked, spun about with feverish haste for a minute by the machine, pushed out clear to resume their leisured progress while the machine jumps on the next piece and works its ordered will upon it. That was the impression if one watched the men filing up to and away from the doctor's hands. It was quite different if attention were concentrated on the doctor alone and the case he handled. That brought instant realization of the human side, the high skill of the swiftly moving fingers, the perfection of knowledge that directed them, the second-cutting haste with which a bandage was stripped off, the tenderness that over-rode the haste as the raw wound and quivering flesh were bared, the sure, unhesitating touch that handled the wound with a maximum of speed finely adjusted to a minimum of hurt, the knowledge that saw in one swift glance what was to be done, the technical skill, instant, exact, and undeviating, that did it. Here, too, was another human side in the men who moved forward one by one into the strong lamp-light to be handled and dealt with, to hear maybe and pretend not to heed the verdict that meant a remaining life to be spent in crippled incompetence, in bed-ridden helplessness; or a sentence that left nothing of hope, that reduced to bare hours in the semi-dark of underground, of cold and damp, of lonely thoughts, the life of a man who a few hours before had been crammed with health and strength and vitality, overflowing with animal fitness and energy. With all these men it appeared to be a point of honor to show nothing of flinching from pain or from fear of the future. All at least bore the pain grimly and stoically, most bore it cheerfully, looked a detached sort of interest at their uncovered wounds, spoke with the doctor lightly or even jestingly. If it was a slight wound there was usually a great anxiety to know if it would be "a Blighty one"; if it were serious, the anxiety was still there, but studiously hidden under an assumed carelessness, and the questioning would be as to whether "it would have to come off" or "is there a chance for me?"

When Kentucky's turn came he moved forward and sat himself on a low box beside the table, and before he was well seated the orderly was slipping off the jacket thrown over his shoulders and buttoned across his chest. The doctor was in his shirt-sleeves, and a dew of perspiration beaded his forehead and shone damp on his face and throat. "Shell, sir," said Kentucky in answer to the quick question as the doctor began rapidly to unwind the bandages on his shoulder. "Dropped in a shell hole next the one I was lying in with another man. That's him," and he nodded to where Pug lay on the other doctor's table. "He's hurt much worse than me. He's a particular chum of mine, sir, and—would you mind, sir?—if you could ask the other doctor he might tell me what Pug's chances are."

"We'll see," said the doctor. "But I'm afraid you've got a nasty hand here yourself," as he carefully unwound the last of the bandage from Kentucky's fingers and gently pulled away the blood-clotted pad from them. "Yes, sir," agreed Kentucky. "But, you see, Pug got it in the leg, and the bearers say that's smashed to flinders, and he's plugged full of other holes as well. I'm rather anxious about him, sir; and if you could ask...."

"Presently," said the doctor, and went on with his work. "What was your job before the war? Will it cripple you seriously to lose that

126

hand; because I'm afraid they'll have to amputate when you go down."

Kentucky was anxiously watching the men at the other table and trying to catch a glimpse of what they were doing. "It doesn't matter so much about that, sir," he said: "and I'm a lot more worried about Pug. He'll lose a leg if he loses anything, and mebbe he mightn't pull through. Couldn't you just have a look at him yourself, sir?"

As it happened, his doctor was called over a minute later to a hurried consultation at the other table. The two doctors conferred hastily, and then Kentucky's doctor came back to finish his bandaging.

"Bad," he said at once in answer to Kentucky's look. "Very bad. Doubtful if it is worth giving him a place in the ambulance. But he has a faint chance. We'll send him down later—when there's room— if he lasts.... There you are ... now the anti-tetanic...." busying himself with the needle "... and off you go to Blighty."

"Thank you, sir," said Kentucky. "And can I stay beside Pug till it's time to move?"

"Yes," said the doctor. "But I'm afraid we'll have to let you walk if you can manage it. There's desperately little room in the ambulances."

"I can walk all right, sir," said Kentucky; and presently, with a label tied to the breast of his jacket, moved aside to wait for Pug's removal from the table. They brought him over presently and carried him into the other room and laid him down there close to the foot of another stair leading to above-ground. Kentucky squatted beside him and leaned over the stretcher. "Are you awake, Pug?" he said softly, and immediately Pug's eyes opened. "Hullo, Kentuck," he said cheerfully. "Yes, I'm awake orright. They wanted to gimme another dose o' that sleep stuff in there, but I tole 'em I wasn't feelin' these holes hurt a bit. I wanted to 'ave a talk to you, y'see, ol' man, an' didn't know if another pill 'ud let me."

"Sure they don't hurt much?" said Kentucky.

"No," said Pug; "but it looks like a wash-out for me, Kentuck."

"Never believe it, boy," said Kentucky, forcing a gayety that was the

127

last thing he actually felt. "We're going down and over to Blighty together."

Pug grinned up at him. "No kid stakes, Kentuck," he said; "or mebbe you don't know. But I 'eard wot them M.O.s was sayin', though they didn't know I did. They said it wasn't worth sendin' me out to the ambulance. You knows wot that means as well as me, Kentuck."

Kentucky was silent. He knew only too well what it meant. Where every stretcher and every place in the ambulances is the precious means of conveyance back to the doctors, and hospitals, and the hope of their saving of the many men who have a chance of that saving, no stretcher and no place dare be wasted to carry back a dying man, merely that he may die in another place. The ones that may be saved take precedence, and those that are considered hopeless must wait until a slackening of the rush allows them to be sent. In one way it may seem cruel, but in the other and larger way it is the more humane and merciful.

"There's always a chance, Pug," said Kentucky, striving to capture hope himself. "Course there is," said Pug. "An' you can bet I'm goin' to fight it out an' cheat them doctors if it can be done, Kentuck. You'll go down ahead o' me, but there ain't so many casualties comin' in now, an' the battalion bein' on the way out will leave less to be casualtied an' more room on the amb'lance. You keep a lookout for me, Kentuck. I might be down at the boat as soon as you yet."

"That's the talk, boy," said Kentucky. A man hobbling on a stick came in from the doctors' room, and, seeing Kentucky, picked his way over the outstretched forms to him. "Hello, Kentuck," he said. "You got your packet passed out to you, then. An' you, too, Pug?" as he caught sight of Pug's face half-hidden in bandages.

"Cheer-oh, Jimmy," said Pug. "Yes, gave me my little sooven-eer all right. An' the worst of it is I'm afraid they've made a mess o' my fatal beauty."

"Never min', Pug," said Jimmy, chuckling and seating himself beside the stretcher. "I see they've lef' your 'andsome boko in action an' fully efficient."

"Wot's yours?" said Pug with interest. "Oh, nothin' much," said the other. "Bit of shrap through the foot. Just good enough for Blighty, an' nothin' else to fuss about. How far did you get?"

128

Pug tried to tell his story, but in spite of himself his voice weakened and slurred, and Kentucky, catching Jimmy's eye, placed his finger on his lips and nodded significantly towards Pug. Jimmy took the hint promptly. "Hullo, some more o' the old crush over there," he said. "I must go'n 'ave a chin-wag with 'em," and he moved off.

"D'you think you could find me a drink, Kentuck?" said Pug; and Kentucky went and got some from an orderly and brought it and held it to the hot lips. After that he made Pug lie quiet, telling him he was sure it was bad for him to be talking; and because the drug still had a certain amount of hold perhaps, Pug half-drowsed and woke and drowsed again. And each time he woke Kentucky spoke quietly and cheerfully to him, and lied calmly, saying it wasn't time for him to go yet—although many others had gone and Kentucky had deliberately missed his turn to go for the sake of remaining beside the broken lad. Most of the walking cases went on at once or in company with stretcher parties, but Kentucky let them go and waited on, hour after hour. His own arm and hand were throbbing painfully, and he was feeling cold and sick and deadly tired. He was not sleepy, and this apparently was unusual, for most of the men there, if their pain was not too great, lay or sat and slept the moment they had the chance. Although many went, the room was always full, because others came as fast. The place was lit by a couple of hanging lamps, and blue wreaths of cigarette smoke curled and floated up past their chimneys and drifted up the stairway. Kentucky sat almost opposite the stair, and the lamplight shone on the steps and on the figures that disappeared up it one by one, their legs and feet tramping up after their heads and bodies had passed out of vision. The ground above had evidently been churned into thin mud, and the water from this ran down the stair, and a solid mass of the thicker mud followed gradually and overflowed step by step under the trampling feet. For an hour Kentucky watched it coming lower and lower, and thought disgustedly of the moment when it would reach the floor and be tramped and spread out over it, thick and slimy and filthy. His back began to ache, and the tiredness to grip and numb him, and his thoughts turned with intolerable longing to the moment when he would get off his mud-encrusted clothes and lie in a clean hospital bed. Every now and then some orderlies and bearers clumped down the stair into the dug-out, and after a little stir of preparation a batch of the wounded would walk or be helped or carried up out into the open to start their journey back to the ambulances. But the cleared space they left quickly filled again with the steady inflow of

129

men who came from the doctors' hands in the other room, and these in their turn settled themselves to wait their turn squatting along the walls or lying patiently on their stretchers. They were all plastered and daubed with wet mud and clay, worn and drooping with pain and fatigue; but all who had a spark of consciousness or energy left were most amazingly cheerful and contented. They smoked cigarettes and exchanged experiences and opinions, and all were most anxious to find out something of how "the show" had gone. It was extraordinary how little they each appeared to know of the fight they had taken such an active part in, how ignorant they were of how well or ill the action had gone as a whole. Some talked very positively, but were promptly questioned or contradicted by others just as positive; others confessed blank ignorance of everything except that they themselves had stayed in some ditch for a certain number of hours, or that the battalion had been "held up" by machine-gun fire; or that the shelling had been "hell." "But if I'd 'a' had to ha' choosed," said one, "I'd ha' sooner been under their shell-fire than ours. The Bosche trenches in front o' us was just blowed out by the roots."

"Never seed no Bosche trenches myself," said another. "I dodged along outer one shell-hole inter another for a bit an' couldn't see a thing for smoke. An' then I copped it and crawled back in an' out more shell-holes. Only dash thing I've seed o' this battle has been shell-holes an' smoke."

"Anyways," put in a man with a bandaged jaw, mumblingly, "if we didn't see much we heard plenty. I didn't think a man's bloomin' ears would 'ave 'eld so much row at onct."

"We got heaps an' heaps o' prisoners," said a man from his stretcher. "I saw that much. We muster took a good bit o' ground to get what I saw myself o' them."

"Hadn't took much where I was," remarked another. "I didn't stir out of the trench we occupied till a crump blew me out in a heap."

"Did any o' you see them Tanks? Lumme, wasn't they a fair treat?..."

Talk of the Tanks spread over all the dug-out. It was plain that they were the feature of the battle. Every man who had seen them had wonder tales to tell; every man who had not seen was thirsting for information from the others. The Tanks were one huge joke. Their actual services were overshadowed by their humor. They drew endless comparisons and similes; the dug-out rippled with laughter and chucklings over their appearance, their uncouth antics and—primest jest of all—the numbers their guns had cut down, the attempts of the Germans to bolt from them, the speed and certainty with which a gust of their machine-gun fire had caught a hustling mob of fugitives, hailed through them, tumbled them in kicking, slaughtered heaps.

In the midst of the talk a sudden heavy crash sounded outside and set the dug-out quivering. A couple more followed, and a few men came down the stairs and stood crowded together on its lower steps and about its foot.

"Pitchin' 'em pretty close," one of these informed the dug-out. "Too close for comfort. An' there's about a dozen chaps lyin' on top there waitin' for stretchers."

Immediately there followed another tremendous crash that set the dug-out rocking like a boat struck by a heavy wave. From above came a confused shouting, and the men on the stair surged back and down a step, while earth fragments rattled and pattered down after them.

In the dug-out some of the men cursed and others laughed and thanked their stars—and the Bosche diggers of the dug-out—that they were so deep under cover. The next shells fell further away, but since the Germans of course knew the exact location of the dug-out, there was every prospect of more close shooting.

Efforts were concentrated on clearing the wounded who lay at the top of the stair in the open and as many of the occupants of the dug-out as possible.

But Kentucky managed to resist or evade being turned out and held his place in the shadows at Pug's head, sat there still and quiet and watched the others come one by one and pass out in batches. And each time Pug stirred and spoke, "You there, Kentuck? Ain't it time you was gone?" told him, "Not yet, boy. Presently." And he noticed with a pang that each time Pug spoke his voice was fainter and weaker. He spoke to an orderly at last, and the doctor came and made a quick examination. With his finger still on Pug's wrist he looked up at Kentucky and slightly shook his head and spoke in a low tone. "Nothing to be done," he said, and rose and passed to where he could do something.

"Kentuck," said Pug very weakly; "collar hold o' that Germ 'elmet o' mine. I got no one at 'ome to send it to ... an' I'd like you to 'av it, chummy ... for a sooven-eer ... o' an ol' pal." Kentucky with an effort steadied his voice and stooped and whispered for a minute. He could just catch a faint answer, "I'm orright, chum. I ain't afeard none ..." and then after a long pause, "Don't you worry 'bout me. I'm orright." And that was his last word.

Kentucky passed up the stair and out into the cold air heavily and almost reluctantly. Even although he could do nothing more, he hated leaving Pug; but room was precious in the dug-out, and the orderlies urged him to be off. He joined a party of several other "walking cases" and a couple of men on stretchers, and with them struck off across the battlefield towards the point on the road which was the nearest the ambulance could approach to the dressing station. The Germans had begun to shell again, and several "crumps" fell near the dug-out. Kentucky, with his mind busied in thoughts of Pug, hardly heeded, but the others of the party expressed an anxiety and showed a nervousness greater than Kentucky had ever noticed before. The explanation was simple, and was voiced by one cheerful casualty on a stretcher. "I've got my dose, an' I'm bound for Blighty," he said, "an' gels chuckin' flowers in the ambulance in Lunnon. If you bloomin' bearers goes cartin' me into the way o' stoppin' another one—strewth, I'll come back an' 'aunt yer. I've 'ad the physic, an' I don't want to go missin' none o' the jam."

They moved slowly across the torn fields and down along the slope towards the road. In the valley they walked in thin, filmy mists, and further on, where low hills rose out of the hollow, camp fires twinkled and winked in scores on the hillsides. And still further, when they rounded a low shoulder and the valley and the hills beyond opened wide to them, the fires increased from scores to hundreds. "Bloomin' Crystal Palis on firework night," said one man, and "Why don't the special constables make 'em draw the blinds an' shade the lights?" said another.

Kentucky saw these things, heard the men's talk, without noting them; and yet the impression must have been deeper and sharper than he knew, for there came a day when he recalled every spot of light and blot of shadow, every curve of hill and mist-shrouded valley, every word and smothered groan and rough jest and laugh, as clearly as if they had been in his eyes and ears a minute before. In the same detached way he saw the bodies of men lying stiff in grotesque, twisted postures or in the peaceful attitudes of quiet sleep, the crawling mists and the lanterns of orderlies and stretcher-bearers searching the field for any still living, heard the weak quavering calls that came out of the mists at intervals like the lonely cries of sheep lost on a mountain crag, the thin, long-drawn "He-e-e-lp" of men too sore stricken to move, calling to guide the rescuers they knew would be seeking them. And in the same fashion, after they came to the ambulances waiting on the broken roadside and he had been helped to the seat beside the driver of one, he noticed how slowly and carefully the man drove and twisted in and out dodging the shell holes; noticed, without then realizing their significance, the legions of men who tramped silently and stolidly, or whistling and singing and blowing on mouth-organs, on their way up to the firing line, the faces emerging white and the rifles glinting out of the darkness into the brightness of the headlights. The car made a wide detour by a road which ran over a portion of ground captured from the Germans a few weeks before. A cold gray light was creeping in before they cleared this ground that already was a swarming hive of British troops, and further than the faint light showed, Kentucky could see and sense parked ranks of wagons, lines of horses, packed camps of men and rows of bivouacs. From there and for miles back the car crept slowly past gun positions and batteries beyond count or reckoning, jolted across the metals of a railway line that was already running into the captured ground, past "dump" after "dump" of ammunition, big shells and little piled in stacks and house-high pyramids, patches of ground floored acre-wide with trench mortar bombs like big footballs, familiar gray boxes of grenades and rifle cartridges, shells again, and yet more shells. "Don't look like we expected to ever lose any o' this ground again," said the driver cheerfully, and Kentucky realized—then and afterwards—just how little it looked like it, and quoted softly to himself, from the Battle Hymn again—"He has sounded forth the trumpet that shall never call retreat." As the light grew and the car passed back to where the road was less damaged or better repaired their speed increased and they ran spattering in the roadside to meet more long columns of men with the brown rifle barrels sloped and swaying evenly above the yellow ranks—"... a fiery gospel writ in rows of burnished steel," murmured Kentucky. "Wot say?" questioned the driver. "Nothing," said Kentucky. "That's the clearin' station ahead there," said the driver. "You'll soon be tucked up safe in a bed now, or pushin' on to the ambulance train and a straight run 'ome to Blighty."

So Kentucky came out of the battle, and stepping down from the ambulance, with an alert orderly attentive at his elbow to help him, took the first step into the swift stages of the journey home, and the long vista of kindness, gentleness, and thoughtful care for which the hospital service is only another name. From here he had nothing to do but sleep, eat, and get well. He was done with battle, and quit of the firing line. But as he came away the war had one more word for his ear, and as he was carried on board the hospital train, the distant guns growled and muttered their last same message to him—"grapes of wrath, of wrath, of wrath."

And after he had lost the last dull rumble of the guns he still bore the memory of their message with him, carried it down to the edge of France, and across the Narrow Seas, and into the sheltered calm of England.

He had been strangely impressed by the fitting of his half-forgotten verses to all he had come through, and their chance but clear coincidence worked oddly on him, and came in the end to be a vital influence in picking the path of his immediate future and leading it utterly away from other plans.

CHAPTER XVI

PLAY OUT THE GAME

Kentucky thought often over the Battle Hymn in the long waking hours of pain and the listless time of convalescence, and since his thoughts came in time to crystallize into words and words are easier to set down than thoughts, here is a talk that he had, many weeks after, when he was almost well again—or rather as well as he would ever be.

The talk was with Larry, with the broken wreck of a Larry who would never, as the doctors told him, walk or stand upright again. Kentucky had finished his convalescing at Larry's home, and the talk came one night when they were alone together in the big dining-room, Larry, thin-faced and claw-handed, on a couch before the fire, Kentucky in a deep armchair. They had chatted idly and in broken snatches of old days, and of those last desperate days in "the Push," and on a chance mention of Pug both had fallen silent for a space.

"Poor Pug," said Larry at last. "Did it ever strike you, Kentuck, what a queer quartette of chums we were, Billy Simson and Pug and you and me?"

"Yes, mighty queer, come to think of it," agreed Kentucky. "And the game handed it out pretty rough for the lot of us—Billy and Pug killed, you like this, and me ..." and he had lifted the stump of a hand bound about with black silk bandages and showing nothing but a thumb and the stump of a finger. "And I figure that out of the lot yours is maybe the worst."

135

"I don't know," said Larry slowly. "I'm well enough off, after all, with a good home and my people asking nothing better than to have the looking after of me. I always think Billy had the hardest luck to be hit again just as he was coming out of it all with a safe and cushy one."

"Anyway," said Kentucky, "it's a sure thing I came out best. I'm crippled, of course, but I'm not right out of action, and can still play a little hand in the game."

"That's right," said Larry heartily. "You're fit enough to tackle the job in his office in my place that the Pater's so keen to have you take—and as I am, selfishly, because the offer carries the condition that you live with us. I hope you've decided to sign on with the firm?"

"I'm going to tell your father to-night," said Kentucky very slowly. "But I'm glad to have the chance to tell you first. I asked him to give me a day to think it over because I wanted to know first if I'd a good-enough reason for refusing——"

"Refusing," Larry said, and almost cried the word.

"When I went out this morning," said Kentucky quietly, "I went to the Red Cross people and had a talk with Kendrick. I showed him I was fit enough for the job and he asked me if I'd take an ambulance car to drive up front."

Larry stared at him. "Up front again," he gasped. "Haven't you had enough of the front?"

"More than enough," said Kentucky gravely. "I'm not going because I like it, any more than I did in the first place. It's just because I think I ought to play out the game."

"God," said Larry. "As if you hadn't done enough. You've got your discharge as unfit. Who would ever blame you for not going back, or dream you ought to go?"

"Only one man," said Kentucky with the glimmer of a smile, "but one that counts a smart lot with me; and he's—myself."

"But it's nonsense," said Larry desperately. "Why, it's not even as if you were one of us. After all, you're American, and this country has no claim, never had a claim, on you. You've done more than your

136

share already. There isn't an earthly reason why you should go again."

"Not even one of us," repeated Kentucky softly. "Well, now, haven't I earned the right to call myself one of you? No, never mind; course I know you didn't mean it that way. But you're wrong otherwise, boy. I'm not an American now. If you folks went to war with America to-morrow, and I was fit to fight, I'd have to fight on your side. There was an oath I took to serve your King, when I enlisted, you'll remember."

"No one would expect an oath like that to bind you to fight against your own people," said Larry quickly.

"In Kentucky, boy," said Kentucky gently, his speech running, as it always did when he was stirred into the slurred, soft "r"-less drawl of his own South, "an oath is an oath, and a promise is little sho't of it. I fought foh yoh country because I thought yoh country was right. But I come at last to fight foh her, because I've got to be proud of her and of belonging to her. And I want to pay the best bit of respect I can think of to those men I fought along with. It just pleases me some to think poor old Pug and Billy and a right smart mo' we knew would like it—I'm going to take out naturalization papers just as soon as I can do it."

"Like it," said Larry, with his eyes glistening; "why, yes, I think they'd like it."

Kentucky hesitated a little, then went on slowly: "And theh's some verses I know that have so't of come to map out a route fo' me to follow. Oveh theh those verses stood right up an' spoke to me. I've thought it oveh quite a lot since, an' it's sure plain to me that I was made to see how close they fitted to what I could see, an' heah, an' undehstand, just so I could use the otheh verses to show me otheh things I could not undehstand. I'd like to tell yo' some of those verses an' how they come in."

He told first the picture he had seen of the German prisoners searching amongst their own heaped dead, while the British guard stood watching them, and the sky flickered with "the fateful lightning" and the guns growled their triumph song; and then went on and repeated the verse of the Battle Hymn, "Mine eyes have seen——"

137

"You see just how exact it fitted," he said. "But it wasn't only in that. Theh were otheh lines"; and he went on to tell of the journey back from the advanced dressing station, the camp fires dotting the hills, the mists crawling in the valley, the lanterns moving to and fro where the bearers still searched for the wounded. "Just see how it came in again," he said, and repeated another verse:

> I have seen Him in the watch-fires of a hundred circling camps,
> They have builded Him an altar in the evening dews and damps,
> I have read His righteous sentence in the dim and flaring lamps,
> His truth is marching on.

"That wasn't all," he went on. "The words fitted 'most everywheh they touched. All along I've neveh quite managed to get so soaked in confidence that we must win as every man I've met in the British Army has been. I've had some doubts at times; but that night I lost them all. It wasn't only seeing the men pouring up into the firing line, an' the sureness of not being driven back that I could figure was in the minds of the higher Commands when they set to building roads an' rails right up into the captured ground; it wasn't only the endless stacks of shells and stuff piled right there on the back doorstep of the battle, and the swarms of guns we came back through. It was something that just spoke plain and clear in my ear, 'He has sounded forth the trumpet that shall never call retreat,' an' I've had no shadow of doubt since but that Germany will go undeh, that theh is nothing left for her but defeat, that she is to be made to pay to the last bitter squeezing of the grapes of wrath for the blood and misery she plunged Europe into. Theh will be no mercy fo' heh. That was told me plain too—'I have read the fiery gospel writ in rows of burnished steel, "As ye deal with My contemners so with you My soul shall deal."' ... Bernhardi an' all his lot writ a fiery enough gospel, but it's cold print beside that other one, that strips the last hope of mercy from His contemners with their gospel of blood and iron and terror and frightfulness." He paused and was silent a little, and then glanced half-shamefacedly from the flickering fire-shadows at Larry.

"Any one else might think I was talkin' like a rantin', crazy, fanatic preacher," he said. "But you an' I, boy, an' most that's been oveh theh, will undehstand, because we've learned a lot mo' than we can eveh tell or speak out loud.... So I've come to believe that all these things fetched home a plain message to me, an' I'd do right to follow the rest of the verses as best I could. 'As He died to make men holy, let us die to make men free,' is straight enough, an' I've got to go on offering my life as long as He sees fit to let me, or until He sees fit to take it."

> He has sounded forth the trumpet that shall never call retreat,
> He is sifting out the hearts of men before His judgment seat,
> O be swift, my soul, to answer Him, be jubilant my feet,
> Our God is marching on!

He was speaking now slowly and low and musingly, almost as if he spoke to himself. "My heart has had some sifting too. It was so easy to take this offeh of yo' father's, and live pleasant an' smooth; an' it was nasty to think about that otheh life, an' the muck and misery of it all. But altho' I could be no ways swift or jubilant about it, I came to allow I'd just go again, an' do what I could."

In the silence that followed they heard the quick slam of an outer door, and a minute later their room door swung open and some one entered briskly, stopped in the half-dark and cried out in a girl's laughing voice, "Why—whatever are you two boys doing in the dark?"

Kentucky had jumped to his feet and was moving round the couch, but Larry's sister spoke imperiously. "Will you sit down, Kentuck? How often have I to tell you that you haven't quite escaped being an invalid yet?"

"Why, now, I thought I'd been discharged fit," said Kentucky, and Larry called, "Come here, Rose, and see if you can persuade this crazy fellow."

Rose came forward into the firelight and made Kentucky sit again, and dropped to a seat on the floor in front of Larry's couch. Kentucky sat back in the shadow looking at her and thinking what a picture she made with her pretty English face framed in a dark close-fitting hat and a heavy fur round her throat with the outside damp clinging and sparkling on it.

"Persuade him," she said, "what to? Wouldn't it be easier for me just to order him?"

"He talks about going back," said Larry. "Out there—to the front again."

139

The girl sat up wide-eyed. "The front," she repeated. "But how—I don't understand—your hand...."

"Not in the firing line," said Kentucky quickly, "I'm not fit for that. But I am fit for Red Cross work."

"It's as bad," said Larry, "if you're working close up, as I know you'd be if you had a chance."

The girl was staring into the flickering fire with set lips. She looked round suddenly and leaned forward and slipped a hand on to Kentucky's knee. "Oh, Ken ... don't, don't go. Stay here with us."

Kentucky's thought flashed out to "over there," where he would move in mud and filth, would be cold and wet and hungry. He saw himself crawling a car along the shell-holed muddy track, his hands stiff with cold, the rain beating and driving in his face, the groans of his load of wounded behind him, the stench of decay and battle in his nostrils, the fear of God and the whistling bullets and roaring shells cold in his heart. And against that was this snug, cozy room and all the life that it stood for ... and the warm touch of the girl's hand on his knee. He wavered a moment while a line hammered swiftly through his mind, "... sifting out the hearts of men...."

Then he spoke quietly, almost casually; but knowing him as they did, both knew that his words were completely final.

"Why, now," he said slowly, "Kendrick, my friend Kendrick of the Red Cross, asked me; and I passed my word, I gave my promise that I'd go."